PUFFIN BOOKS

DEMIGODS AND MAGICIANS

*Also available as a graphic novel

rickriordanmythmaster.co.uk

DEMIGODS AND MAGICIANS

RICK RIORDAN

PUFFIN

PUFFIN BOOKS

UK | USA | Canada | Ireland | Australia
India | New Zealand | South Africa

Puffin Books is part of the Penguin Random House group of companies
whose addresses can be found at global.penguinrandomhouse.com.

www.penguin.co.uk
www.puffin.co.uk
www.ladybird.co.uk

The Son of Sobek, *The Staff of Serapis* and *The Crown of Ptolemy* first published
respectively in the USA by Disney • Hyperion, an imprint of Disney Book Group,
and in Great Britain by Puffin Books as digital editions in 2013, 2014 and 2015

First published in this collection in Great Britain by Puffin Books 2016

004

Text copyright © Rick Riordan, 2013, 2014, 2015, 2016
Hieroglyph art by Michelle Gengaro-Kokmen

The moral right of the author and illustrator has been asserted

Typeset in 11.5/18.5 pt Adobe Caslon Pro

Printed in Great Britain by Clays Ltd, St Ives plc

A CIP catalogue record for this book is available from the British Library

ISBN: 978-0-141-36728-6

All correspondence to:
Puffin Books, Penguin Random House Children's
80 Strand, London WC2R ORL

Contents

THE
SON
OF
SOBEK

GETTING EATEN BY a giant crocodile was bad enough.

The kid with the glowing sword only made my day worse.

Maybe I should introduce myself.

I'm Carter Kane – part-time high-school freshman, part-time magician, full-time worrier about all the Egyptian gods and monsters who are constantly trying to kill me.

Okay, that last part is an exaggeration. Not *all* the gods want me dead. Just a lot of them – but that kind of goes with the territory, since I'm a magician in the House of Life. We're like the police for Ancient Egyptian supernatural forces, making sure they don't cause too much havoc in the modern world.

Anyway, on this particular day I was tracking down a

rogue monster on Long Island. Our scryers had been sensing magical disturbances in the area for several weeks. Then the local news started reporting that a large creature had been sighted in the ponds and marshes near the Montauk Highway – a creature that was eating the wildlife and scaring the locals. One reporter even called it the Long Island Swamp Monster. When mortals start raising the alarm, you know it's time to check things out.

Normally my sister, Sadie, or some of our other initiates from Brooklyn House would've come with me. But they were all at the First Nome in Egypt for a week-long training session on controlling cheese demons (yes, they're a real thing – believe me, you don't want to know), so I was on my own.

I hitched our flying reed boat to Freak, my pet griffin, and we spent the morning buzzing around the south shore, looking for signs of trouble. If you're wondering why I didn't just ride on Freak's back, imagine two hummingbird-like wings beating faster and more powerfully than helicopter blades. Unless you want to get shredded, it's really better to ride in the boat.

Freak had a pretty good nose for magic. After a couple of hours on patrol, he shrieked, 'FREEEEEEK!' and banked hard to the left, circling over a green marshy inlet between two neighbourhoods.

'Down there?' I asked.

Freak shivered and squawked, whipping his barbed tail nervously.

I couldn't see much below us – just a brown river glittering in the hot summer air, winding through swamp grass and clumps of gnarled trees until it emptied into Moriches Bay. The area looked a bit like the Nile Delta back in Egypt, except here the wetlands were surrounded on both sides by residential neighbourhoods with row after row of grey-roofed houses. Just to the north, a line of cars inched along the Montauk Highway – vacationers escaping the crowds in the city to enjoy the crowds in the Hamptons.

If there really was a carnivorous swamp monster below us, I wondered how long it would be before it developed a taste for humans. If that happened . . . well, it was surrounded by an all-you-can-eat buffet.

'Okay,' I told Freak. 'Set me down by the riverbank.'

As soon as I stepped out of the boat, Freak screeched and zoomed into the sky, the boat trailing behind him.

'Hey!' I yelled after him, but it was too late.

Freak is easily spooked. Flesh-eating monsters tend to scare him away. So do fireworks, clowns and the smell of Sadie's weird British Ribena drink. (Can't blame him on that last one. Sadie grew up in London and developed some pretty strange tastes.)

I would have to take care of this monster problem, then whistle for Freak to pick me up once I was done.

I opened my backpack and checked my supplies: some enchanted rope, my curved ivory wand, a lump of wax for making a magical *shabti* figurine, my calligraphy set and a healing potion my friend Jaz had brewed for me a while back. (She knew that I got hurt a lot.)

There was just one more thing I needed.

I concentrated and reached into the Duat. Over the last few months, I'd got better at storing emergency provisions in the shadow realm – extra weapons, clean clothes, Fruit by the Foot and chilled six-packs of root beer – but sticking my hand into a magical dimension still felt weird, like pushing through layers of cold, heavy curtains. I closed my fingers round the hilt of my sword and pulled it out – a weighty *khopesh* with a blade curved like a question mark. Armed with my sword and wand, I was all set for a stroll through the swamp to look for a hungry monster. Oh, joy!

I waded into the water and immediately sank to my knees. The river bottom felt like congealed stew. With every step, my shoes made such rude noises – *suck-plop*, *suck-plop* – that I was glad Sadie wasn't with me. She never would've stopped laughing.

Even worse, making this much noise, I knew I wouldn't be able to sneak up on any monsters.

Mosquitoes swarmed me. Suddenly I felt nervous and alone.

Could be worse, I told myself. *I could be studying cheese demons.*

But I couldn't quite convince myself. In a nearby neighbourhood, I heard kids shouting and laughing, probably playing some kind of game. I wondered what that would be like – being a normal kid, hanging out with my friends on a summer afternoon.

The idea was so nice I got distracted. I didn't notice the ripples in the water until fifty yards ahead of me something broke the surface – a line of leathery blackish-green bumps. Instantly it submerged again, but I knew what I was dealing with now. I'd seen crocodiles before, and this was a freakishly big one.

I remembered El Paso, the winter before last, when my

sister and I had been attacked by the crocodile god Sobek. That *wasn't* a good memory.

Sweat trickled down my neck.

'Sobek,' I murmured, 'if that's you, messing with me again, I swear to Ra . . .'

The croc god had promised to leave us alone now that we were tight with his boss, the sun god. Still . . . crocodiles get hungry. Then they tend to forget their promises.

No answer from the water. The ripples subsided.

When it came to sensing monsters, my magic instincts weren't very sharp, but the water in front of me seemed much darker. That meant either it was deep, or something large was lurking under the surface.

I almost hoped it *was* Sobek. At least then I stood a chance of talking to him before he killed me. Sobek loved to boast.

Unfortunately, it wasn't him.

The next microsecond, as the water erupted around me, I realized too late that I should've brought the entire Twenty-first Nome to help me. I registered glowing yellow eyes as big as my head, the glint of gold jewellery round a massive neck. Then monstrous jaws opened – ridges of crooked teeth and an expanse of pink maw wide enough to gulp down a garbage truck.

And the creature swallowed me whole.

*

Imagine being shrink-wrapped upside down inside a gigantic slimy garbage bag with no air. Being in the monster's belly was like that, only hotter and smellier.

For a moment I was too stunned to do anything. I couldn't believe I was still alive. If the crocodile's mouth had been smaller, he might have snapped me in half. As it was, he had gulped me down in a single Carter-sized serving, so I could look forward to being slowly digested.

Lucky, right?

The monster started thrashing around, which made it hard to think. I held my breath, knowing that it might be my last. I still had my sword and wand, but I couldn't use them with my arms pinned to my side. I couldn't reach any of the stuff in my bag.

Which left only one answer: a word of power. If I could think of the right hieroglyphic symbol and speak it aloud, I could summon some industrial-strength, wrath-of-the-gods-type magic to bust my way out of this reptile.

In theory: a great solution.

In practice: I'm not so good at words of power even in the best of situations. Suffocating inside a dark, smelly reptile gullet wasn't helping me focus.

You can do this, I told myself.

After all the dangerous adventures I'd had, I couldn't die like this. Sadie would be devastated. Then, once she got over her grief, she'd track down my soul in the Egyptian afterlife and tease me mercilessly for how stupid I'd been.

My lungs burned. I was blacking out. I picked a word of power, summoned all my concentration and prepared to speak.

Suddenly the monster lurched upward. He roared, which sounded really weird from the inside, and his throat contracted round me like I was being squeezed from a toothpaste tube. I shot out of the creature's mouth and tumbled into the marsh grass.

Somehow I got to my feet. I staggered around, half blind, gasping and covered with crocodile goo, which smelled like a scummy fish tank.

The surface of the river churned with bubbles. The crocodile was gone, but standing in the marsh about twenty feet away was a teenage guy in jeans and a faded orange T-shirt that said CAMP something. I couldn't read the rest. He looked a little older than me – maybe seventeen – with tousled black hair and sea-green eyes. What really caught my attention was his sword – a straight double-edged blade glowing with faint bronze light.

I'm not sure which of us was more surprised.

For a second, Camper Boy just stared at me. He noted my *khopesh* and wand, and I got the feeling that he actually *saw* these things as they were. Normal mortals have trouble seeing magic. Their brains can't interpret it, so they might look at my sword, for instance, and see a baseball bat or a walking stick.

But this kid . . . he was different. I figured he must be a magician. The only problem was I'd met most of the magicians in the North American nomes, and I'd never seen this guy before. I'd also never seen a sword like that. Everything about him seemed . . . *un-Egyptian*.

'The crocodile,' I said, trying to keep my voice calm and even. 'Where did it go?'

Camper Boy frowned. 'You're welcome.'

'What?'

'I stuck that croc in the rump.' He mimicked the action with his sword. 'That's why it vomited you up. So, you're welcome. What were you doing in there?'

I'll admit I wasn't in the best mood. I smelled. I hurt. And, yeah, I was a little embarrassed: the mighty Carter Kane, head of Brooklyn House, had been disgorged from a croc's mouth like a giant hairball.

'I was resting,' I snapped. 'What do you *think* I was doing? Now, who are you, and why are you fighting my monster?'

'*Your* monster?' The guy trudged towards me through the water. He didn't seem to have any trouble with the mud. 'Look, man, I don't know who you are, but that crocodile has been terrorizing Long Island for weeks. I take that kind of personally, as this is my home turf. A few days ago, it ate one of our pegasi.'

A jolt went up my spine like I'd backed into an electric fence. 'Did you say *pegasi*?'

He waved the question aside. 'Is it your monster or not?'

'I don't own it!' I growled. 'I'm trying to *stop* it! Now, where –'

'The croc headed that way.' He pointed his sword to the south. 'I would already be chasing it, but you surprised me.'

He sized me up, which was disconcerting since he was half a foot taller. I still couldn't read his T-shirt except for the word camp. Round his neck hung a leather strap with some colourful clay beads, like a kid's arts-and-crafts project. He wasn't carrying a magician's pack or a wand. Maybe he kept them in the Duat? Or maybe he was just a delusional mortal who'd accidentally found a magic sword and thought he was a superhero. Ancient relics can really mess with your mind.

Finally he shook his head. 'I give up. Son of Ares? You've

got to be a half-blood, but what happened to your sword? It's all bent.'

'It's a *khopesh*.' My shock was rapidly turning to anger. 'It's supposed to be curved.'

But I wasn't thinking about the sword.

Camper Boy had just called me a *half-blood*? Maybe I hadn't heard him right. Maybe he meant something else. But my dad was African-American. My mom was white. *Half-blood* wasn't a word I liked.

'Just get out of here,' I said, gritting my teeth. 'I've got a crocodile to catch.'

'Dude, *I* have to catch the crocodile,' he insisted. 'Last time you tried, it ate you. Remember?'

My fingers tightened round my sword hilt. 'I had everything under control. I was about to summon a fist –'

For what happened next, I take full responsibility.

I didn't mean it. Honestly. But I was angry. And, as I may have mentioned, I'm not always good at channelling words of power. While I was in the crocodile's belly, I'd been preparing to summon the Fist of Horus: a giant glowing blue hand that can pulverize doors, walls and pretty much anything else that gets in your way. My plan had been to punch my way out of the monster. Gross, yes, but hopefully effective.

I guess that spell was still in my head, ready to be triggered like a loaded gun. Facing Camper Boy, I was furious, not to mentioned dazed and confused; so when I meant to say the English word *fist* it came out in Ancient Egyptian instead: *khefa*.

Such a simple hieroglyph:

You wouldn't think it could cause so much trouble.

As soon as I spoke the word, the symbol blazed in the air between us. A giant fist the size of a dishwasher shimmered into existence and slammed Camper Boy into the next county.

I mean I *literally* punched him out of his shoes. He rocketed from the river with a loud *suck-plop!* And the last thing I saw was his bare feet achieving escape velocity as he flew backwards and disappeared from sight.

No, I didn't feel good about it. Well . . . maybe a tiny bit good. But I also felt mortified. Even if the guy was a jerk, magicians weren't supposed to go around sucker-punching kids into orbit with the Fist of Horus.

'Oh, great.' I hit myself on the forehead.

I started to wade across the marsh, worried that I'd actually killed the guy. 'Man, I'm sorry!' I yelled, hoping he could hear me. 'Are you –?'

The wave came out of nowhere.

A twenty-foot wall of water slammed into me and pushed me back into the river. I came up spluttering, a horrible taste like fish food in my mouth. I blinked the gunk out of my eyes just in the time to see Camper Boy leaping towards me ninja-style, his sword raised.

I lifted my *khopesh* to deflect the blow. I just managed to keep my head from being cleaved in half, but Camper Boy was strong and quick. As I reeled backwards, he struck again and again. Each time, I was able to parry, but I could tell I was outmatched. His blade was lighter and quicker, and – yes, I'll admit it – he was a better swordsman.

I wanted to explain that I'd made a mistake. I wasn't really his enemy. But I needed all my concentration just to keep from getting sliced down the middle.

Camper Boy, however, had no trouble talking.

'Now I get it,' he said, swinging at my head. 'You're some kind of monster.'

CLANG! I intercepted the strike and staggered back.

'I'm not a monster,' I managed.

To beat this guy, I'd have to use more than just a sword.

The problem was I didn't want to hurt him. Despite the fact that he was trying to chop me into a Kane-flavoured barbecue sandwich, I still felt bad for starting the fight.

He swung again, and I had no choice. I used my wand this time, catching his blade in the crook of ivory and channelling a burst of magic straight up his arm. The air between us flashed and crackled. Camper Boy stumbled back. Blue sparks of sorcery popped around him, as if my spell didn't know quite what to do with him. Who *was* this guy?

'You said the crocodile was *yours*.' Camper Boy scowled, anger blazing in his green eyes. 'You lost your pet, I suppose. Maybe you're a spirit from the Underworld, come through the Doors of Death?'

Before I could even process that question, he thrust out his free hand. The river reversed course and swept me off my feet.

I managed to get up, but I was getting really tired of drinking swamp water. Meanwhile Camper Boy charged again, his sword raised for the kill. In desperation, I dropped my wand. I thrust my hand into my backpack, and my fingers closed round the piece of rope.

I threw it and yelled the command word '*TAS!*' – *bind* – just as Camper Boy's bronze blade cut into my wrist.

My whole arm erupted in agony. My vision tunnelled. Yellow spots danced before my eyes. I dropped my sword and clutched my wrist, gasping for breath, everything forgotten except the excruciating pain.

In the back of my mind, I knew Camper Boy could kill me easily. For some reason he didn't. A wave of nausea made me double over.

I forced myself to look at the wound. There was a lot of blood, but I remembered something Jaz had told me once in the infirmary at Brooklyn House: cuts usually looked a lot worse than they were. I hoped that was true. I fished a piece of papyrus out of my backpack and pressed it against the wound as a makeshift bandage.

The pain was still horrible, but the nausea became more manageable. My thoughts started to clear, and I wondered why I hadn't been skewered yet.

Camper Boy was sitting nearby in waist-deep water, looking dejected. My magic rope had wrapped round his sword arm, then lashed his hand to the side of his head. Unable to let go of his sword, he looked like he had a single reindeer antler sprouting next to his ear. He tugged at the rope with his free hand, but of course he couldn't make any progress.

Finally he just sighed and glared at me. 'I'm really starting to hate you.'

'Hate *me*?' I protested. 'I'm gushing blood here! And you started all this by calling me a half-blood!'

'Oh, please.' Camper Boy rose unsteadily, his sword antenna making him top-heavy. 'You can't be mortal. If you were, my sword would've passed right through you. If you're not a spirit or a monster, you've got to be a half-blood. A rogue demigod from Kronos's army, I'd guess.'

Most of what this guy said, I didn't understand. But one thing sank in.

'So when you said "half-blood" . . .'

He stared at me like I was an idiot. 'I meant *demigod*. Yeah. What did you *think* I meant?'

I tried to process that. I'd heard the term *demigod* before, but it wasn't an Egyptian concept. Maybe this guy was sensing that I was bound to Horus, that I could channel the god's power . . . but why did he describe everything so strangely?

'What are you?' I demanded. 'Part combat magician, part water elementalist? What nome are you with?'

The kid laughed bitterly. 'Dude, I don't know what you're talking about. I don't hang out with gnomes. Satyrs, sometimes. Even Cyclopes. But not gnomes.'

The blood loss must have been making me dizzy. His words bounced around in my head like lottery balls: *Cyclopes*, *satyrs*, *demigods*, *Kronos*. Earlier he'd mentioned Ares. That was a Greek god, not Egyptian.

I felt like the Duat was opening underneath me, threatening to pull me into the depths. *Greek . . . not Egyptian.*

An idea started forming in my mind. I didn't like it. In fact, it scared the holy Horus out of me.

Despite all the swamp water I'd swallowed, my throat felt dry. 'Look,' I said, 'I'm sorry about hitting you with that fist spell. It was an accident. But the thing I don't understand . . . it should have killed you. It didn't. That doesn't make sense.'

'Don't sound so disappointed,' he muttered. 'But, while we're on the subject, you should be dead too. Not many people can fight me that well. And my sword should have vaporized your crocodile.'

'For the last time, it's not *my* crocodile.'

'Okay, whatever.' Camper Boy looked dubious. 'The point is I stuck that crocodile pretty good, but I just made it angry. Celestial bronze should've turned it to dust.'

'Celestial bronze?'

Our conversation was cut short by a scream from the nearby neighbourhood – the terrified voice of a kid.

My heart did a slow roll. I really was an idiot. I'd forgotten why we were here.

I locked eyes with Camper Boy. 'We've got to stop the crocodile.'

'Truce,' he suggested.

'Yeah,' I said. 'We can continue killing each other after the crocodile is taken care of.'

'Deal. Now, could you please untie my sword hand from my head? I feel like a freaking unicorn.'

I won't say we trusted each other, but at least now we had a common cause. He summoned his shoes out of the river – I had no idea how – and put them on. Then he helped me bind my hand with a strip of linen and waited while I swigged down half of my healing potion.

After that, I felt good enough to race after him towards the sound of the screaming.

I thought I was in pretty good shape – what with combat magic practice, hauling heavy artefacts and playing basketball with Khufu and his baboon friends (baboons don't mess around when it comes to hoops). Nevertheless, I had to struggle to keep up with Camper Boy.

Which reminded me, I was getting tired of calling him that.

'What's your name?' I asked, wheezing as I ran behind him.

He gave me a cautious glance. 'I'm not sure I should tell you. Names can be dangerous.'

He was right, of course. Names held power. A while back, my sister, Sadie, had learned my *ren*, my secret name, and it still caused me all sorts of anxiety. Even with someone's common name, a skilled magician could work all kinds of mischief.

'Fair enough,' I said. 'I'll go first. I'm Carter.'

I guess he believed me. The lines around his eyes relaxed a bit.

'Percy,' he offered.

That struck me as an unusual name – British, maybe, though the kid spoke and acted very much like an American.

We jumped a rotten log and finally made it out of the marsh. We'd started climbing a grassy slope towards the nearest houses when I realized more than one voice was screaming up there now. Not a good sign.

'Just to warn you,' I told Percy, 'you can't kill the monster.'

'Watch me,' Percy grumbled.

'No, I mean it's *immortal*.'

'I've heard that before. I've vaporized plenty of *immortals* and sent them back to Tartarus.'

Tartarus? I thought.

Talking to Percy was giving me a serious headache. It reminded me of the time my dad took me to Scotland for one of his Egyptology lectures. I'd tried to talk with some of the locals and I knew they were speaking English, but every other sentence seemed to slip into an alternate language – different words, different pronunciations – and I'd wonder what the heck they were saying. Percy was like that. He and I *almost* spoke the same language – magic, monsters, et cetera. But his vocabulary was completely wrong.

'No,' I tried again, halfway up the hill. 'This monster is a *petsuchos* – a son of Sobek.'

'Who's Sobek?' he asked.

'Lord of crocodiles. Egyptian god.'

That stopped him in his tracks. He stared at me, and I could swear the air between us turned electric. A voice, very deep in my mind, said: *Shut up. Don't tell him any more.*

Percy glanced at the *khopesh* I'd retrieved from the river, then the wand in my belt. 'Where are you from? Honestly.'

'Originally?' I asked. 'Los Angeles. Now I live in Brooklyn.'

That didn't seem to make him feel any better. 'So this monster, this *pet-suck-o* or whatever –'

'*Petsuchos*,' I said. 'It's a Greek word, but the monster is

Egyptian. It was like the mascot of Sobek's temple, worshipped as a living god.'

Percy grunted. 'You sound like Annabeth.'

'Who?'

'Nothing. Just skip the history lesson. How do we kill it?'

'I told you –'

From above came another scream, followed by a loud *CRUNCH*, like the sound made by a metal compactor.

We sprinted to the top of the hill, then hopped the fence of somebody's backyard and ran into a residential cul-de-sac.

Except for the giant crocodile in the middle of the street, the neighbourhood could have been Anywhere, USA. Ringing the cul-de-sac were half a dozen single-storey homes with well-kept front lawns, economy cars in the driveways, mailboxes at the kerb, flags hanging above the front porches.

Unfortunately, the all-American scene was kind of ruined by the monster, who was busily eating a green Prius hatchback with a bumper sticker that read MY POODLE IS SMARTER THAN YOUR HONOUR STUDENT. Maybe the *petsuchos* thought the Toyota was another crocodile, and he was asserting his dominance. Maybe he just didn't like poodles and/or honour students.

Whatever the case, on dry land the crocodile looked even scarier than he had in the water. He was about forty feet long, as tall as a delivery truck, with a tail so massive and powerful it overturned cars every time it swished. His skin glistened blackish green and gushed water that pooled around his feet. I remembered Sobek once telling me that his divine sweat created the rivers of the world. Yuck. I guessed this monster had the same holy perspiration. Double yuck.

The creature's eyes glowed with a sickly yellow light. His jagged teeth gleamed white. But the weirdest thing about him was his bling. Round his neck hung an elaborate collar of gold chains and enough precious stones to buy a private island.

The necklace was how I had realized the monster was a *petsuchos*, back at the marsh. I'd read that the sacred animal of Sobek wore something just like it back in Egypt, though what the monster was doing in a Long Island neighbourhood, I had no idea.

As Percy and I took in the scene, the crocodile clamped down and bit the green Prius in half, spraying glass and metal and pieces of airbag across the lawns.

As soon as he dropped the wreckage, half a dozen kids appeared from nowhere – apparently they'd been hiding behind some of the other cars – and charged the monster, screaming at the top of their lungs.

I couldn't believe it. They were just elementary-age kids, armed with nothing but water balloons and Super Soakers. I guessed that they were on summer break and had been cooling off with a water fight when the monster interrupted them.

There were no adults in sight. Maybe they were all at work. Maybe they were inside, passed out from fright.

The kids looked angry rather than scared. They ran round the crocodile, lobbing water balloons that splashed harmlessly against the monster's hide.

Useless and stupid? Yes. But I couldn't help admiring their bravery. They were trying their best to face down a monster that had invaded their neighbourhood.

Maybe they saw the crocodile for what it was. Maybe their mortal brains made them think it was an escaped elephant from the zoo, or a crazed FedEx delivery driver with a death wish.

Whatever they saw, they were in danger.

My throat closed up. I thought about my initiates back at Brooklyn House, who were no older than these kids, and my protective 'big brother' instincts kicked in. I charged into the street, yelling, 'Get away from it! Run!'

Then I threw my wand straight at the crocodile's head. '*Sa-mir!*'

The wand hit the croc on the snout, and blue light rippled across his body. All over the monster's hide, the hieroglyph for *pain* flickered:

Everywhere it appeared, the croc's skin smoked and sparked, causing the monster to writhe and bellow in annoyance.

The kids scattered, hiding behind ruined cars and mail-boxes. The *petsuchos* turned his glowing yellow eyes on me.

At my side, Percy whistled under his breath. 'Well, you got his attention.'

'Yeah.'

'You sure we can't kill him?' he asked.

'Yeah.'

The crocodile seemed to be following our conversation. His yellow eyes flicked back and forth between us, as if deciding which of us to eat first.

'Even if you *could* destroy his body,' I said, 'he would just reappear somewhere nearby. That necklace? It's enchanted with the power of Sobek. To beat the monster, we have to get that necklace off. Then the *petsuchos* should shrink back into a regular crocodile.'

'I hate the word *should*,' Percy muttered. 'Fine. I'll get the necklace. You keep him occupied.'

'Why do *I* get to keep him occupied?'

'Because you're more annoying,' Percy said. 'Just try not to get eaten again.'

'ROARR!' the monster bellowed, his breath like a seafood restaurant's dumpster.

I was about to argue that Percy was *plenty* annoying, but I didn't get the chance. The *petsuchos* charged, and my new comrade-in-arms sprinted to one side, leaving me right in the path of destruction.

First random thought: *Getting eaten twice in one day would be very embarrassing.*

Out of the corner of my eye, I saw Percy dashing towards the monster's right flank. I heard the mortal kids come out from their hiding places, yelling and throwing more water balloons like they were trying to protect me.

The *petsuchos* lumbered towards me, his jaws opening to snap me up.

And I got angry.

I'd faced the worst Egyptian gods. I'd plunged into the Duat and trekked across the Land of Demons. I'd stood at the very shores of Chaos. I was *not* going back down to an overgrown gator.

The air crackled with power as my combat avatar formed round me – a glowing blue exoskeleton in the shape of Horus.

It lifted me off the ground until I was suspended in the middle of a twenty-foot-tall, hawk-headed warrior. I stepped forward, bracing myself, and the avatar mimicked my stance.

Percy yelled, 'Holy Hera! What the –?'

The crocodile slammed into me.

He nearly toppled me. His jaws closed round my avatar's free arm, but I slashed the hawk warrior's glowing blue sword at the crocodile's neck.

Maybe the *petsuchos* couldn't be killed. I was at least hoping to cut through the necklace that was the source of his power.

Unfortunately, my swing went wide. I hit the monster's shoulder, cleaving his hide. Instead of blood, he spilled sand, which is pretty typical for Egyptian monsters. I would have enjoyed seeing him disintegrate completely, but no such luck. As soon as I yanked my blade free, the wound started closing and the sand slowed to a trickle. The crocodile whipped his head from side to side, pulling me off my feet and shaking me by the arm like a dog with a chew toy.

When he let me go, I sailed straight into the nearest house and smashed through the roof, leaving a hawk-warrior-shaped crater in someone's living room. I really hoped I hadn't just flattened some defenceless mortal in the middle of watching *Dr Phil*.

My vision cleared, and I saw two things that irritated me. First, the crocodile was charging me again. Second, my new friend Percy was just standing in the middle of the street, staring at me in shock. Apparently my combat avatar had startled him so much he'd forgotten his part of the plan.

'What the creeping crud is *that*?' he demanded. 'You're inside a giant glowing chicken-man!'

'Hawk!' I yelled.

I decided that if I survived this day I would have to make sure this guy never met Sadie. They'd probably take turns insulting me for the rest of eternity. 'A little help here?'

Percy unfroze and ran towards the croc. As the monster closed in on me, I kicked him in the snout, which made him sneeze and shake his head long enough for me to extricate myself from the ruined house.

Percy jumped on the creature's tail and ran up his spine. The monster thrashed around, his hide shedding water all over the place, but somehow Percy managed to keep his footing. The guy must have practised gymnastics or something.

Meanwhile, the mortal kids had found some better ammunition – rocks, scrap metal from the wrecked cars, even a few tyre irons – and were hurling the stuff at the monster. I didn't want the crocodile turning his attention towards them.

'HEY!' I swung my *khopesh* at the croc's face – a good solid strike that should've taken off his lower jaw. Instead, he somehow snapped at the blade and caught it in his mouth. We ended up wrestling for the blue glowing sword as it sizzled in his mouth, making his teeth crumble to sand. That couldn't have felt good, but the croc held on, tugging against me.

'Percy!' I shouted. 'Any time now!'

Percy lunged for the necklace. He grabbed hold and started hacking at the gold links, but his bronze sword didn't make a dent.

Meanwhile, the croc was going crazy trying to yank away my sword. My combat avatar started to flicker.

Summoning an avatar is a short-term thing, like sprinting at top speed. You can't do it for very long, or you'll collapse. Already I was sweating and breathing hard. My heart raced. My reservoirs of magic were being severely depleted.

'Hurry,' I told Percy.

'Can't cut it!' he said.

'A clasp,' I said. 'There's gotta be one.'

As soon as I said that, I spotted it – at the monster's throat, a golden cartouche encircling the hieroglyphs that spelled sobek. 'There – on the bottom!'

Percy scrambled down the necklace, climbing it like a net, but at that moment my avatar collapsed. I dropped to the ground, exhausted and dizzy. The only thing that saved my life was that the crocodile had been pulling at my avatar's sword. When the sword disappeared, the monster lurched backwards and stumbled over a Honda.

The mortal kids scattered. One dived under a car, only to have the car disappear – smacked into the air by the croc's tail.

Percy reached the bottom of the necklace and hung on for dear life. His sword was gone. Probably he'd dropped it.

Meanwhile, the monster regained his footing. The good news: he didn't seem to notice Percy. The bad news: he *definitely* noticed me, and he looked mightily torqued off.

I didn't have the energy to run, much less summon magic to fight. At this point, the mortal kids with their water balloons and rocks had more of a chance of stopping the croc than I did.

In the distance, sirens wailed. Somebody had called the police, which didn't exactly cheer me up. It just meant more mortals were racing here as fast as they could to volunteer as crocodile snacks.

I backed up to the kerb and tried – ridiculously – to stare down the monster. 'Stay, boy.'

The crocodile snorted. His hide shed water like the grossest fountain in the world, making my shoes slosh as I walked. His lamp-yellow eyes filmed over, maybe from happiness. He knew I was done for.

I thrust my hand into my backpack. The only thing I found was a clump of wax. I didn't have time to build a proper *shabti*, but I had no better idea. I dropped my pack and started working the wax furiously with both hands, trying to soften it.

'Percy?' I called.

'I can't unlock the clasp!' he yelled. I didn't dare take my eyes off the croc's, but in my peripheral vision I could see Percy pounding his fist against the base of the necklace. 'Some kind of magic?'

That was the smartest thing he'd said all afternoon (not that he'd said a lot of smart things to choose from). The clasp was a hieroglyphic cartouche. It would take a magician to figure it out and open it. Whatever and whoever Percy was, he was no magician.

I was still shaping the clump of wax, trying to make it into a figurine, when the crocodile decided to stop savouring the moment and just eat me. As he lunged, I threw my *shabti*, only half formed, and barked a command word.

Instantly the world's most deformed hippopotamus sprang to life in midair. It sailed headfirst into the crocodile's left nostril and lodged there, kicking its stubby back legs.

Not exactly my finest tactical move, but having a hippo shoved up his nose must have been sufficiently distracting. The crocodile hissed and stumbled, shaking his head, as Percy dropped off and rolled away, barely avoiding the crocodile's stomping feet. He ran to join me at the kerb.

I stared in horror as my wax creature, now a living (though very misshapen) hippo, tried to either wriggle free of the croc's nostril or work its way further into the reptile's sinus cavity – I wasn't sure which.

The crocodile whipped round, and Percy grabbed me just in time, pulling me out of its trampling path.

We jogged to the opposite end of the cul-de-sac, where the mortal kids had gathered. Amazingly, none of them seemed to be hurt. The crocodile kept thrashing and wiping out homes as it tried to clear its nostril.

'You okay?' Percy asked me.

I gasped for air but nodded weakly.

One of the kids offered me his Super Soaker. I waved him off.

'You guys,' Percy told the kids, 'you hear those sirens? You've got to run down the road and stop the police. Tell them it's too dangerous up here. Stall them!'

For some reason, the kids listened. Maybe they were just happy to have something to do, but, from the way Percy spoke, I got the feeling he was used to rallying outnumbered troops. He sounded a bit like Horus – a natural commander.

After the kids raced off, I managed to say, 'Good call.'

Percy nodded grimly. The crocodile was still distracted by its nasal intruder, but I doubted the *shabti* would last much longer. Under that much stress, the hippo would soon melt back to wax.

'You've got some moves, Carter,' Percy admitted. 'Anything else in your bag of tricks?'

'Nothing,' I said dismally. 'I'm running on empty. But if I can get to that clasp I think I can open it.'

Percy sized up the *petsuchos*. The cul-de-sac was filling with water that poured from the monster's hide. The sirens were getting louder. We didn't have much time.

'Guess it's my turn to distract the croc,' he said. 'Get ready to run for that necklace.'

'You don't even have your sword,' I protested. 'You'll die!'

Percy managed a crooked smile. 'Just run in there as soon as it starts.'

'As soon as *what* starts?'

Then the crocodile sneezed, launching the wax hippo across Long Island. The *petsuchos* turned towards us, roaring in anger, and Percy charged straight at him.

As it turned out, I didn't need to ask what kind of distraction Percy had in mind. Once it started, it was pretty obvious.

He stopped in front of the crocodile and raised his arms. I figured he was planning some kind of magic, but he spoke no command words. He had no staff or wand. He just stood there and looked up at the crocodile as if to say, *Here I am! I'm tasty!*

The crocodile seemed momentarily surprised. If nothing

35

else, we would die knowing that we'd confused this monster many, many times.

Croc sweat kept pouring off his body. The brackish stuff was up to the kerb now, up to our ankles. It sloughed into the storm drains but just continued spilling from the croc's skin.

Then I saw what was happening. As Percy raised his arms, the water began swirling counterclockwise. It started around the croc's feet and quickly built speed until the whirlpool encompassed the entire cul-de-sac, spinning strongly enough that I could feel it pulling me sideways.

By the time I realized I'd better start running, the current was already too fast. I'd have to reach the necklace some other way.

One last trick, I thought.

I feared the effort might literally burn me up, but I summoned my final bit of magical energy and transformed into a falcon – the sacred animal of Horus.

Instantly, my vision was a hundred times sharper. I soared upward, above the rooftops, and the entire world switched to high-definition 3D. I saw the police cars only a few blocks away, the kids standing in the middle of the street, waving them down. I could make out every slimy bump and pore on the crocodile's hide. I could see each hieroglyph on the clasp of the necklace. And I could see just how impressive Percy's magic trick was.

The entire cul-de-sac was engulfed in a hurricane. Percy stood at the edge, unmoved, but the water was churning so fast now that even the giant crocodile lost his footing. Wrecked cars scraped along the pavement. Mailboxes were pulled out of lawns and swept away. The water increased in volume as well as speed, rising up and turning the entire neighbourhood into a liquid centrifuge.

It was my turn to be stunned. A few moments ago, I'd decided Percy was no magician. Yet I'd never seen a magician who could control so much water.

The crocodile stumbled and struggled, shuffling in a circle with the current.

'Any time now,' Percy muttered through gritted teeth. Without my falcon hearing, I never would've heard him through the storm, but I realized he was talking to me.

I remembered I had a job to do. No one, magician or otherwise, could control that kind of power for long.

I folded my wings and dived for the crocodile. When I reached the necklace's clasp, I turned back to human and grabbed hold. All around me, the hurricane roared. I could barely see through the swirl of mist. The current was so strong now it tugged at my legs, threatening to pull me into the flood.

I was *so* tired. I hadn't felt this pushed beyond my limits since I'd fought the Chaos lord, Apophis himself.

I ran my hand over the hieroglyphs on the clasp. There had to be a secret to unlocking it.

The crocodile bellowed and stomped, fighting to stay on its feet. Somewhere to my left, Percy yelled in rage and frustration, trying to keep up the storm, but the whirlpool was starting to slow.

I had a few seconds at best until the crocodile broke free and attacked. Then Percy and I would both be dead.

I felt the four symbols that made up the god's name:

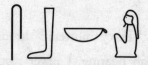

The last symbol didn't actually represent a sound, I knew. It was the hieroglyph for *god*, indicating that the letters in front of it – *SBK* – stood for a deity's name.

When in doubt, I thought, *hit the* god *button*.

I pushed the fourth symbol, but nothing happened.

The storm was failing. The crocodile started to turn against the current, facing Percy. Out of the corner of my eye, through the haze and mist, I saw Percy drop to one knee.

My fingers passed over the third hieroglyph – the wicker basket (Sadie always called it the 'teacup') that stood for the *K* sound. The hieroglyph felt slightly warm to the touch – or was that my imagination?

No time to think. I pressed it. Nothing happened.

The storm died. The crocodile bellowed in triumph, ready to feed.

I made a fist and slammed the basket hieroglyph with all my strength. This time the clasp made a satisfying *click* and sprang open. I dropped to the pavement, and several hundred pounds of gold and gems spilled on top of me.

The crocodile staggered, roaring like the guns of a battleship. What was left of the hurricane scattered in an explosion of wind, and I shut my eyes, ready to be smashed flat by the body of a falling monster.

Suddenly, the cul-de-sac was silent. No sirens. No crocodile roaring. The mound of gold jewellery disappeared. I was lying on my back in mucky water, staring up at the empty blue sky.

Percy's face appeared above me. He looked like he'd just run a marathon through a typhoon, but he was grinning.

'Nice work,' he said. 'Get the necklace.'

'The necklace?' My brain still felt sluggish. Where had all that gold gone? I sat up and put my hand on the pavement. My fingers closed round the strand of jewellery, now normal-sized . . . well, at least *normal* for something that could fit round the neck of an average crocodile.

'The – the monster,' I stammered. 'Where –?'

Percy pointed. A few feet away, looking very disgruntled, was a baby crocodile not more than three feet long.

'You can't be serious,' I said.

'Maybe somebody's abandoned pet?' Percy shrugged. 'You hear about those on the news sometimes.'

I couldn't think of a better explanation, but how had a baby croc got hold of a necklace that turned him into a giant killing machine?

Down the street, voices started yelling, 'Up here! There's these two guys!'

It was the mortal kids. Apparently they'd decided the danger was over. Now they were leading the police straight towards us.

'We have to go.' Percy scooped up the baby crocodile, clenching one hand round his little snout. He looked at me. 'You coming?'

Together, we ran back to the swamp.

*

Half an hour later, we were sitting in a diner off the Montauk Highway. I'd shared the rest of my healing potion with Percy, who for some reason insisted on calling it *nectar*. Most of our wounds had healed.

We'd tied the crocodile in the woods on a makeshift leash, just until we could figure out what to do with it. We'd cleaned up as best we could, but we still looked like we'd taken a shower in a malfunctioning car wash. Percy's hair was swept to one side and tangled with pieces of grass. His orange shirt was ripped down the front.

I'm sure I didn't look much better. I had water in my shoes, and I was still picking falcon feathers out of my shirt sleeves (hasty transformations can be messy).

We were too exhausted to talk as we watched the news on the television above the counter. Police and firefighters had responded to a freak sewer event in a local neighbourhood. Apparently pressure had built up in the drainage pipes, causing a massive explosion that unleashed a flood and eroded the soil so badly several houses on the cul-de-sac had collapsed. It was a miracle that no residents had been injured. Local kids were telling some wild stories about the Long Island Swamp Monster, claiming it had caused all the damage during a fight with two teenage boys, but of course the officials didn't believe this. The reporter admitted, however, that the damaged houses looked like 'something very large had sat on them'.

'A freak sewer accident,' Percy said. 'That's a first.'

'For you, maybe,' I grumbled. 'I seem to cause them everywhere I go.'

'Cheer up,' he said. 'Lunch is on me.'

He dug into the pockets of his jeans and pulled out a ballpoint pen. Nothing else.

'Oh . . .' His smile faded. 'Uh, actually . . . can you conjure up money?'

So, naturally, lunch was on *me*. I *could* pull money out of thin air, since I kept some stored in the Duat along with my other emergency supplies; so in no time we had cheeseburgers and fries in front of us, and life was looking up.

'Cheeseburgers,' Percy said. 'Food of the gods.'

'Agreed,' I said, but when I glanced over at him I wondered if he was thinking the same thing I was: that we were referring to *different* gods.

Percy inhaled his burger. Seriously, this guy could eat. 'So, the necklace,' he said between bites. 'What's the story?'

I hesitated. I still had no clue where Percy came from or

what he was, and I wasn't sure I wanted to ask. Now that we'd fought together, I couldn't help but trust him. Still, I sensed we were treading on dangerous ground. Everything we said could have serious implications – not just for the two of us but maybe for everyone we knew.

I felt sort of like I had two winters ago, when my uncle Amos explained the truth about the Kane family heritage – the House of Life, the Egyptian gods, the Duat, everything. In a single day, my world expanded tenfold and left me reeling.

Now I was standing at the edge of another moment like that. But if my world expanded tenfold *again* I was afraid my brain might explode.

'The necklace is enchanted,' I said at last. 'Any reptile that wears it turns into the next *petsuchos*, the Son of Sobek. Somehow that little crocodile got it round his neck.'

'Meaning someone *put* it round his neck,' Percy said.

I didn't want to think about that, but I nodded reluctantly.

'So, who?' he asked.

'Hard to narrow it down,' I said. 'I've got a lot of enemies.'

Percy snorted. 'I can relate to that. Any idea *why*, then?'

I took another bite of my cheeseburger. It was good, but I had trouble concentrating on it.

'Someone wanted to cause trouble,' I speculated. 'I think maybe . . .' I studied Percy, trying to judge how much I should say. 'Maybe they wanted to cause trouble that would get our attention. *Both* of our attention.'

Percy frowned. He drew something in his ketchup with a French fry – not a hieroglyph. Some kind of non-English letter. Greek, I guessed.

'The monster had a Greek name,' he said. 'It was eating pegasi in my . . .' He hesitated.

'In your home turf,' I finished. 'Some kind of camp, judging from your shirt.'

He shifted on his bar stool. I still couldn't believe he was talking about pegasi as if they were real, but I remembered one time at Brooklyn House, maybe a year back, when I was certain I saw a winged horse flying over the Manhattan skyline. At the time, Sadie had told me I was hallucinating. Now, I wasn't so sure.

Finally Percy faced me. 'Look, Carter. You're not nearly as annoying as I thought. And we made a good team today, but –'

'You don't want to share your secrets,' I said. 'Don't worry. I'm not going to ask about your camp. Or the powers you have. Or any of that.'

He raised an eyebrow. 'You're not curious?'

'I'm *totally* curious. But until we figure out what's going on I think it's best we keep some distance. If someone – some*thing* – unleashed that monster here, knowing it would draw both of our attention –'

'Then maybe that someone wanted us to meet,' he finished. 'Hoping bad things would happen.'

I nodded. I thought about the uneasy feeling I'd had in my gut earlier – the voice in my head warning me not to tell Percy anything. I'd come to respect the guy, but I still sensed that we weren't meant to be friends. We weren't meant to be anywhere *close* to each other.

A long time ago, when I was just a little kid, I'd watched my mom do a science experiment with some of her college students.

Potassium and water, she'd told them. *Separate, completely harmless. But together –*

She dropped the potassium into a beaker of water, and *ka-blam!* The students jumped back as a miniature explosion rattled all the vials in the lab.

Percy was water. I was potassium.

'But we've met now,' Percy said. 'You know I'm out here on Long Island. I know you live in Brooklyn. If we went searching for each other –'

'I wouldn't recommend it,' I said. 'Not until we know more. I need to look into some things on, uh, my side – try to figure out who was behind this crocodile incident.'

'All right,' Percy agreed. 'I'll do the same on my side.'

He pointed at the *petsuchos* necklace, which was glinting just inside my backpack. 'What do we to do about that?'

'I can send it somewhere safe,' I promised. 'It won't cause trouble again. We deal with relics like this a lot.'

'*We*,' Percy said. 'Meaning, there's a lot of . . . you guys?'

I didn't answer.

Percy put up his hands. 'Fine. I didn't ask. I have some friends back at Ca– uh, back on my side who would love tinkering with a magic necklace like that, but I'm going to trust you here. Take it.'

I didn't realize I'd been holding my breath until I exhaled. 'Thanks. Good.'

'And the baby crocodile?' he asked.

I managed a nervous laugh. 'You want it?'

'Gods, no.'

'I can take it, give it a good home.' I thought about our big pool at Brooklyn House. I wondered how our giant magic crocodile, Philip of Macedonia, would feel about having a little friend. 'Yeah, it'll fit right in.'

Percy didn't seem to know what to think of that. 'Okay, well . . .' He held out his hand. 'Good working with you, Carter.'

We shook. No sparks flew. No thunder boomed. But I still couldn't escape the feeling that we'd opened a door, meeting like this – a door that we might not be able to close.

'You too, Percy.'

He stood to go. 'One more thing,' he said. 'If this somebody, whoever threw us together . . . if he's an enemy to both of us – what if we *need* each other to fight him? How do I contact you?'

I considered that. Then I made a snap decision. 'Can I write something on your hand?'

He frowned. 'Like your phone number?'

'Uh . . . well, not exactly.' I took out my stylus and a vial of magic ink. Percy held out his palm. I drew a hieroglyph there – the Eye of Horus. As soon as the symbol was complete, it flared blue, then vanished.

'Just say my name,' I told him, 'and I'll hear you. I'll know where you are, and I'll come meet you. But it will only work once, so make it count.'

Percy considered his empty palm. 'I'm trusting you that this isn't some sort of magical tracking device.'

'Yeah,' I said. 'And I'm trusting that when you call me you won't be luring me into some kind of ambush.'

He stared at me. Those stormy green eyes really were kind of scary. Then he smiled, and he looked like a regular teenager, without a care in the world.

'Fair enough,' he said. 'See you when I see you, C–'

'Don't say my name!'

'Just teasing.' He pointed at me and winked. 'Stay strange, my friend.'

Then he was gone.

An hour later, I was back aboard my airborne boat with the baby crocodile and the magic necklace as Freak flew me home to Brooklyn House.

Now, looking back on it, the whole thing with Percy seems so unreal I can hardly believe it actually happened.

I wonder how Percy summoned that whirlpool, and what the heck *Celestial bronze* is. Most of all, I keep rolling one word around in my mind: *demigod*.

I have a feeling that I could find some answers if I looked hard enough, but I'm afraid of what I might discover.

For the time being, I think I'll tell Sadie about this and no one else. At first she'll think I'm kidding. And, of course, she'll give me grief, but she also knows when I'm telling the truth. As annoying as she is, I trust her (though I would never say that to her face).

Maybe she'll have some ideas about what we should do.

Whoever brought Percy and me together, whoever orchestrated our crossing paths . . . it smacks of Chaos. I can't help thinking this was an experiment to see what kind of havoc would result. Potassium and water. Matter and antimatter.

Fortunately, things turned out okay. The *petsuchos* necklace is safely locked away. Our new baby crocodile is splashing around happily in our pool.

But next time . . . well, I'm afraid we might not be so lucky.

Somewhere there's a kid named Percy with a secret hieroglyph on his hand. And I have a feeling that sooner or later I'll wake up in the middle of the night and hear one word, spoken urgently in my mind:

Carter.

THE
STAFF
OF
SERAPIS

UNTIL SHE SPOTTED the two-headed monster, Annabeth didn't think her day could get any worse.

She'd spent all morning doing catch-up work for school. (Skipping classes on a regular basis to save the world from monsters and rogue Greek gods was seriously messing up her grades.) Then she'd turned down a movie with her boyfriend, Percy, and some of their friends so she could try out for a summer internship at a local architecture firm. Unfortunately, her brain had been mush. She was pretty sure she'd flubbed the interview.

Finally, around four in the afternoon, she'd trudged through Washington Square Park on her way to the subway station and stepped in a fresh pile of cow manure.

She glared at the sky. 'Hera!'

The other pedestrians gave her funny looks, but Annabeth didn't care. She was tired of the goddess's practical jokes. Annabeth had done *so* many quests for Hera, but still the Queen of Heaven left presents from her sacred animal right where Annabeth could step in them. The goddess must have had a herd of stealth cows patrolling Manhattan.

By the time Annabeth made it to the West Fourth Street station, she was cranky and exhausted and just wanted to catch the F train uptown to Percy's place. It was too late for the movie, but maybe they could get dinner or something.

Then she spotted the monster.

Annabeth had seen some crazy stuff before, but this beastie definitely made her 'What Were the Gods Thinking?' list. It looked like a lion and a wolf lashed together, wedged butt-first into a hermit-crab shell.

The shell itself was a rough brown spiral, like a waffle cone – about six feet long with a jagged seam down the middle, as if it had been cracked in half, then glued back together. Sprouting from the top were the forelegs and head of a grey wolf on the left, a golden-maned lion on the right.

The two animals didn't look happy about sharing a shell. They dragged it behind them down the platform, weaving left and right as they tried to pull in different directions.

They snarled at one another in irritation. Then both of them froze and sniffed the air.

Commuters streamed past. Most manoeuvred round the monster and ignored it. Others just frowned or looked annoyed.

Annabeth had seen the Mist in action many times before, but she was always amazed by how the magical veil could distort mortal vision, making even the fiercest monster look like something explainable – a stray dog, or maybe a homeless person wrapped in a sleeping bag.

The monster's nostrils flared. Before Annabeth could decide what to do, both heads turned and glared directly at her.

Annabeth's hand went for her knife. Then she remembered she didn't have one. At the moment, her most deadly weapon was her backpack, which was loaded with heavy architecture books from the public library.

She steadied her breathing. The monster stood about thirty feet away.

Taking on a lion-wolf-crab in the middle of a crowded subway station wasn't her first choice, but, if she had to, she would. She was a child of Athena.

She stared down the beast, letting it know she meant business.

'Bring it on, Crabby,' she said. 'I hope you've got a high tolerance for pain.'

The lion and wolf heads bared their fangs. Then the floor rumbled. Air rushed through the tunnel as a train arrived.

The monster snarled at Annabeth. She could've sworn it had a look of regret in its eyes, as if thinking, *I would love to rip you to tiny pieces, but I have business elsewhere.*

Then Crabby turned and bounded off, dragging its huge shell behind. It disappeared up the stairs, heading for the A train.

For a moment, Annabeth was too stunned to move. She'd rarely seen a monster leave a demigod alone like that. Given the chance, monsters almost *always* attacked.

If this two-headed hermit crab had something more important to do than kill her, Annabeth wanted to know what it was. She couldn't just let the monster go, pursuing its nefarious plans and riding public transportation for free.

She glanced wistfully at the F train that would've taken her uptown to Percy's place. Then she ran up the stairs after the monster.

Annabeth jumped on board just as the doors were closing. The train pulled away from the platform and plunged into darkness.

Overhead lights flickered. Commuters rocked back and forth. Every seat was filled. A dozen more passengers stood, swaying as they clung to the handrails and poles.

Annabeth couldn't see Crabby until somebody at the front yelled, 'Watch it, freak!'

The wolf-lion-crab was pushing its way forward, snarling at the mortals, but the commuters just acted regular-New-York-subway annoyed. Maybe they saw the monster as a random drunk guy.

Annabeth followed.

As Crabby prised open the doors to the next car and clambered through, Annabeth noticed its shell was glowing faintly.

Had it been doing that before? Around the monster swirled red neon symbols – Greek letters, astrological signs and picture writing. *Egyptian hieroglyphs.*

A chill spread between Annabeth's shoulder blades. She remembered something Percy had told her a few weeks ago – about an encounter he'd had that seemed so impossible she'd assumed he was joking.

But now . . .

She pushed through the crowd, following Crabby into the next car.

The creature's shell was definitely glowing brighter now. As Annabeth got closer, she started to get nauseous. She felt a warm tugging sensation in her gut, as if she had a fishhook in her belly button, pulling her towards the monster.

Annabeth tried to steady her nerves. She had devoted her life to studying Ancient Greek spirits, beasts and daimons. Knowledge was her most important weapon. But this two-headed crab thing – she had no frame of reference for it. Her internal compass was spinning uselessly.

She wished she had backup. She had her cell phone, but, even if she could get reception in the tunnel, whom would she call? Most other demigods didn't carry phones. The signals attracted monsters. Percy was way uptown. The majority of her friends were back at Camp Half-Blood on the north shore of Long Island.

Crabby kept shoving its way towards the front of the train.

By the time Annabeth caught up with it in the next car, the monster's aura was so strong that even the mortals had started to notice. Many gagged and hunched over in their seats, as if someone had opened a locker full of spoiled lunches. Others fainted onto the floor.

Annabeth felt so queasy she wanted to retreat, but the

fishhook sensation kept tugging at her navel, reeling her towards the monster.

The train rattled into the Fulton Street station. As soon as the doors opened, every commuter who was still conscious stumbled out. Crabby's wolf head snapped at one lady, catching her bag in its teeth as she tried to flee.

'Hey!' Annabeth yelled.

The monster let the woman go.

Both sets of eyes fixed on Annabeth as if thinking, *Do you have a death wish?*

Then it threw back its heads and roared in harmony. The sound hit Annabeth like an ice pick between the eyes. The windows of the train shattered. Mortals who had passed out were startled back to consciousness. Some managed to crawl out of the doors. Others tumbled through broken windows.

Through blurred vision, Annabeth saw the monster crouched on its mismatched forelegs, ready to pounce.

Time slowed. She was dimly aware of the shattered doors closing, the now-empty train pulling out of the station. Had the conductor not realized what was happening? Was the train running on autopilot?

Only ten feet away from it now, Annabeth noticed new details about the monster. Its red aura seemed brightest along the seam in its shell. Glowing Greek letters and Egyptian hieroglyphs spewed out like volcanic gas from a deep-sea fissure. The lion's left foreleg was shaved above the paw, tattooed with a series of small black stripes. Stuck inside the wolf's left ear was an orange price tag that read $99.99.

Annabeth gripped the strap of her backpack. She was ready to swing it at the monster, but it wouldn't make much of a weapon. Instead, she relied on her usual tactic when facing a stronger enemy. She started talking.

'You're made of two different parts,' she said. 'You're like . . . pieces of a statue that came to life. You've been fused together?'

It was total conjecture, but the lion's growl made Annabeth think she'd hit the mark. The wolf nipped at the lion's cheek as if telling it to shut up.

'You're not used to working together,' Annabeth guessed. 'Mr Lion, you've got an ID code on your leg. You were an artefact in a museum. Maybe the Met?'

The lion roared so loudly Annabeth's knees wobbled.

'I guess that's a yes. And you, Mr Wolf . . . that sticker on your ear . . . you were for sale in some antiques shop?'

The wolf snarled and took a step towards her.

Meanwhile, the train kept tunnelling under the East River. Cold wind swirled through the broken windows and made Annabeth's teeth chatter.

All her instincts told her to run, but her joints felt as if they were dissolving. The monster's aura kept getting brighter, filling the air with misty symbols and bloody light.

'You . . . you're getting stronger,' Annabeth noted. 'You're heading somewhere, aren't you? And the closer you get –'

The monster's heads roared again in harmony. A wave of red energy rippled through the car. Annabeth had to fight to stay conscious.

Crabby stepped closer. Its shell expanded, the fissure down the centre burning like molten iron.

'Hold up,' Annabeth croaked. 'I – I get it now. You're not finished yet. You're looking for another piece. A third head?'

The monster halted. Its eyes glinted warily, as if to say, *Have you been reading my diary?*

Annabeth's courage rose. Finally she was getting the measure of her enemy. She'd met lots of three-headed creatures before. When it came to mythical beings, *three* was sort of a magic number. It made sense that this monster would have another head.

Crabby had been some kind of statue, divided into pieces. Now something had awakened it. It was trying to put itself back together.

Annabeth decided she couldn't let that happen. Those glowing red hieroglyphs and Greek letters floated around it like the burning cord of a fuse, radiating magic that felt fundamentally *wrong*, as though it were slowly dissolving Annabeth's cell structure.

'You're not exactly a Greek monster, are you?' she ventured. 'Are you from Egypt?'

Crabby didn't like that comment. It bared its fangs and prepared to spring.

'Whoa, boy,' she said. 'You're not at full strength yet, are you? Attack me now, and you'll lose. After all, you two don't trust each other.'

The lion tilted its head and growled.

Annabeth feigned a look of shock. 'Mr Lion! How can you say that about Mr Wolf?'

The lion blinked.

The wolf glanced at the lion and snarled suspiciously.

'And, Mr Wolf!' Annabeth gasped. 'You shouldn't use that kind of language about your friend!'

The two heads turned on each other, snapping and

howling. The monster staggered as its forelegs went in different directions.

Annabeth knew she'd only bought herself a few seconds. She racked her brain, trying to figure out what this creature was and how she could defeat it, but it didn't match anything she could remember from her lessons at Camp Half-Blood.

She considered getting behind it, maybe trying to break its shell, but before she could the train slowed. They pulled into the High Street station, the first Brooklyn stop.

The platform was strangely empty, but a flash of light by the exit stairwell caught Annabeth's eye. A young blonde girl in white clothes was swinging a wooden staff, trying to hit a strange animal that weaved around her legs, barking angrily. From the shoulders up, the creature looked like a black Labrador retriever, but its back end was nothing but a rough tapered point, like a calcified tadpole tail.

Annabeth had time to think: *The third piece.*

Then the blonde girl whacked the dog across its snout. Her staff flared with golden light, and the dog hurtled backwards – straight through a broken window into the far end of Annabeth's subway car.

The blonde girl followed it. She leaped in through the closing doors just as the train pulled out of the station.

For a moment they all just stood there – two girls and two monsters.

Annabeth studied the other girl at the opposite end of the car, trying to assess her threat level.

The newcomer wore white linen trousers and a matching blouse, kind of like a karate uniform. Her steel-tipped combat boots looked like they could inflict damage in a fight. Slung over her left shoulder was a blue nylon backpack with a curved ivory stick – a boomerang? – hanging from the strap. But the girl's most intimidating weapon was her white wooden staff – about five feet long, carved with the head of an eagle, the whole length glowing like Celestial bronze.

Annabeth met the girl's eyes, and a feeling of déjà vu rocked her.

Karate Girl couldn't have been older than thirteen. Her eyes were brilliant blue, like a child of Zeus's. Her long blonde hair was streaked with purple highlights. She looked very much like a child of Athena – ready for combat, quick and alert and fearless. Annabeth felt as if she were seeing herself from four years ago, around the time she first met Percy Jackson.

Then Karate Girl spoke and shattered the illusion.

'Right.' She blew a strand of purple hair out of her face. 'Because my day wasn't barmy enough already.'

British, Annabeth thought. But she didn't have time to ponder that.

The dog-tadpole and Crabby had been standing in the centre of the car, about fifteen feet apart, staring at each other in amazement. Now they overcame their shock. The dog howled – a triumphant cry, like *I found you!* And the lion-wolf-crab lunged to meet it.

'Stop them!' Annabeth yelled.

She leaped onto Crabby's back, and its front paws collapsed from the extra weight.

The other girl yelled something like: '*Mar!*'

A series of golden hieroglyphs blazed in the air:

The dog creature staggered backwards, retching as if it had swallowed a billiard ball.

Annabeth struggled to keep Crabby down, but the beast was twice her weight. It pushed up on its forelegs, trying to throw her. Both heads turned to snap at her face.

Fortunately she'd harnessed plenty of wild pegasi at Camp Half-Blood. She managed to keep her balance while slipping off her backpack. She smacked twenty pounds of architecture books into the lion's head, then looped her shoulder strap through the wolf's maw and yanked it like a bit.

Meanwhile, the train burst into the sunlight. They rattled along the elevated rails of Queens, fresh air blowing through the broken windows and glittering bits of glass dancing across the seats.

Out of the corner of her eye, Annabeth saw the black dog shake off its fit of retching. It lunged at Karate Girl, who whipped out her ivory boomerang and blasted the monster with another golden flash.

Annabeth wished she could summon golden flashes. All she had was a stupid backpack. She did her best to subdue Crabby, but the monster seemed to get stronger by the second while the thing's red aura weakened Annabeth. Her head felt stuffed with cotton. Her stomach twisted.

She lost track of time as she wrestled the creature. She only knew she couldn't let it combine with that dog-headed thing. If the monster turned into a complete three-headed whatever-it-was, it might be impossible to stop.

The dog lunged again at Karate Girl. This time it knocked her down. Annabeth, distracted, lost her grip on the crab monster, and it threw her off – slamming her head into the edge of a seat.

Her ears rang as the creature roared in triumph. A wave of red-hot energy rippled through the car. The train pitched sideways, and Annabeth went weightless.

'Up you come,' said a girl's voice. 'We have to move.'

Annabeth opened her eyes. The world was spinning. Emergency sirens wailed in the distance.

She was lying flat on her back in some prickly weeds. The blonde girl from the train leaned over her, tugging on her arm.

Annabeth managed to sit up. She felt as if someone was hammering hot nails into her ribcage. As her vision cleared, she realized she was lucky to be alive. About fifty yards away, the subway train had toppled off the track. The cars lay sideways in a broken, steaming zigzag of wreckage that reminded Annabeth of a drakon carcass (unfortunately, she'd seen several of those).

She spotted no wounded mortals. Hopefully they'd all fled the train at the Fulton Street station. But still – what a disaster.

Annabeth recognized where she was: Rockaway Beach. A few hundred feet to the left, vacant plots and bent chain-link fences gave way to a yellow sand beach dotted with tar and trash. The sea churned under a cloudy sky. To Annabeth's right, past the train tracks, stood a row of apartment towers so dilapidated they might've been make-believe buildings fashioned from old refrigerator boxes.

'Yoo-hoo.' Karate Girl shook her shoulder. 'I know you're probably in shock, but we need to go. I don't fancy being questioned by the police with *this* thing in tow.'

The girl scooted to her left. Behind her on the broken tarmac, the black Labrador monster flopped like a fish out of water, its muzzle and paws bound in glowing golden rope.

Annabeth stared at the younger girl. Round her neck glinted a chain with a silver amulet – a symbol like an Egyptian ankh crossed with a gingerbread man.

At her side lay her staff and her ivory boomerang – both carved with hieroglyphs and pictures of strange, very *un-Greek* monsters.

'Who *are* you?' Annabeth demanded.

A smile tugged at the corner of the girl's mouth. 'Usually I don't give my name to strangers. Magical vulnerabilities and all that. But I have to respect someone who fights a two-headed monster with nothing but a rucksack.' She offered her hand. 'Sadie Kane.'

'Annabeth Chase.'

They shook.

'Lovely to meet you, Annabeth,' Sadie said. 'Now, let's take our dog for a walk, shall we?'

They left just in time.

Within minutes, emergency vehicles had surrounded the train wreck, and a crowd of spectators gathered from the nearby apartment buildings.

Annabeth felt more nauseous than ever. Red spots danced before her eyes, but she helped Sadie drag the dog creature backwards by its tail into the sand dunes. Sadie seemed to take pleasure in pulling the monster over as many rocks and broken bottles as she could find.

The beast snarled and wriggled. Its red aura glowed more brightly, while the golden rope dimmed.

Normally Annabeth liked walking on the beach. The ocean reminded her of Percy. But today she was hungry and exhausted. Her backpack felt heavier by the moment, and the dog creature's magic made her want to hurl.

Also, Rockaway Beach was a dismal place. A massive hurricane had blown through more than a year ago, and the damage was still obvious. Some of the apartment buildings in the distance had been reduced to shells, their boarded-up windows and breeze-block walls covered in graffiti. Rotted timber, chunks of tarmac and twisted metal littered the beach. The pylons of a destroyed pier jutted up out of the water. The sea itself gnawed resentfully at the shore as if to say, *Don't ignore me. I can always come back and finish the job.*

Finally they reached a derelict ice-cream truck half sunken in the dunes. Painted on the side, faded pictures of long-lost tasty treats made Annabeth's stomach howl in protest.

'Gotta stop,' she muttered.

She dropped the dog monster and staggered over to the truck, then slid down with her back against the passenger's door.

Sadie sat cross-legged, facing her. She rummaged around in her own backpack and brought out a cork-stoppered ceramic vial.

'Here.' She handed it to Annabeth. 'It's yummy. Drink.'

Annabeth studied the vial warily. It felt heavy and warm, as if it were full of hot coffee. 'Uh . . . this won't unleash any golden flashes of *ka-bam* in my face?'

Sadie snorted. 'It's just a healing potion, silly. A friend of mine, Jaz, brews the best in the world.'

Annabeth still hesitated. She'd sampled potions before, brewed by the children of Hecate. Usually they tasted like pond-scum soup, but at least they were made to work on demigods. Whatever was in this vial, it definitely wasn't.

'I'm not sure I should try,' she said. 'I'm . . . not like you.'

'*No one* is like me,' Sadie agreed. 'My amazingness is unique. But if you mean you're not a magician, well, I can *see* that. Usually we fight with staff and wand.' She patted the carved white pole and the ivory boomerang lying next to her. 'Still, I think my potions should work on you. You wrestled a monster. You survived that train wreck. You *can't* be normal.'

Annabeth laughed weakly. She found the other girl's brashness sort of refreshing. 'No, I'm definitely not normal. I'm a demigod.'

'Ah.' Sadie tapped her fingers on her curved wand. 'Sorry, that's a new one on me. A *demon god*?'

'Demigod,' Annabeth corrected. 'Half god, half mortal.'

'Oh, right.' Sadie exhaled, clearly relieved. 'I've hosted Isis in my head quite a few times. Who's *your* special friend?'

'My – no. I don't *host* anybody. My mother is a Greek goddess, Athena.'

'Your mother.'

'Yeah.'

'A goddess. A *Greek* goddess.'

'Yeah.' Annabeth noticed that her new friend had gone pale. 'I guess you don't have that kind of thing, um, where you come from.'

'Brooklyn?' Sadie mused. 'No. I don't think so. Or London. Or Los Angeles. I don't recall meeting Greek *demigods* in any of those places. Still, when one has dealt with magical baboons, goddess cats and dwarfs in Speedos, one can't be surprised very easily.'

Annabeth wasn't sure she'd heard right. 'Dwarfs in Speedos?'

'Mmm.' Sadie glanced at the dog monster, still writhing in its golden bonds. 'But here's the rub. A few months ago my mum gave me a warning. She told me to beware of other gods and other types of magic.'

The vial in Annabeth's hands seemed to grow warmer. 'Other gods. You mentioned Isis. She's the Egyptian goddess of magic. But . . . she's not your mom?'

'No,' Sadie said. 'I mean, yes. Isis is the goddess of Egyptian magic. But she's not my mum. My mum's a ghost. Well . . . she was a magician in the House of Life, like me, but then she died, so –'

'Just a sec.' Annabeth's head throbbed so badly she figured nothing could make it worse. She uncorked the potion and drank it down.

She'd been expecting pond-scum consommé, but it actually tasted like warm apple juice. Instantly, her vision cleared. Her stomach settled.

'Wow,' she said.

'Told you.' Sadie smirked. 'Jaz is quite the apothecary.'

'So you were saying . . . House of Life. Egyptian magic. You're like the kid my boyfriend met.'

Sadie's smile eroded. 'Your boyfriend . . . met someone like me? Another magician?'

A few feet away, the dog creature snarled and struggled. Sadie didn't appear concerned, but Annabeth was worried about how dimly the magic rope was glowing now.

'This was a few weeks ago,' Annabeth said. 'Percy told me a crazy story about meeting a boy out near Moriches Bay. Apparently this kid used hieroglyphs to cast spells. He helped Percy battle a big crocodile monster.'

'The Son of Sobek!' Sadie blurted. 'But my *brother* battled that monster. He didn't say anything about –'

'Is your brother's name Carter?' Annabeth asked.

An angry golden aura flickered around Sadie's head – a

halo of hieroglyphs that resembled frowns, fists and dead stick men.

'As of this moment,' Sadie growled, 'my brother's name is Punching Bag. Seems he hasn't been telling me everything.'

'Ah.' Annabeth had to fight the urge to scoot away from her new friend. She feared those glowing angry hieroglyphs might explode. 'Awkward. Sorry.'

'Don't be,' Sadie said. 'I'll rather enjoy bashing my brother's face in. But first tell me everything – about yourself, demigods, Greeks and whatever it might have to do with our evil canine friend here.'

Annabeth told her what she could.

Usually she wasn't so quick to trust, but she'd had a lot of experience reading people. She liked Sadie immediately: the combat boots, the purple highlights, the attitude . . . In Annabeth's experience, untrustworthy people weren't so up-front about wanting to bash someone's face in. They certainly didn't help an unconscious stranger and offer a healing potion.

Annabeth described Camp Half-Blood. She recounted some of her adventures battling gods and giants and Titans. She explained how she'd spotted the two-headed lion-wolf-crab at the West Fourth Street station and decided to follow it.

'So here I am,' Annabeth summed up.

Sadie's mouth quivered. She looked as if she might start yelling or crying. Instead, she broke down in a fit of the giggles.

Annabeth frowned. 'Did I say something funny?'

'No, no . . .' Sadie snorted. 'Well . . . it is a *bit* funny. I mean, we're sitting on the beach talking about Greek gods. And a camp for demigods, and –'

'It's all true!'

'Oh, I believe you. It's too ridiculous *not* to be true. It's just that each time my world gets stranger, I think: *Right. We're at maximum oddness now. At least I know the full extent of it.* First, I find out my brother and I are descended from the pharaohs and have magic powers. All right. No problem. Then I find out my dead father has merged his soul with Osiris and become the lord of the dead. Brilliant! Why not? Then my uncle takes over the House of Life and oversees hundreds of magicians around the world. Then my boyfriend turns out to be a hybrid magician boy/immortal god of funerals. And all the while I'm thinking, *Of course! Keep calm and carry on! I've adjusted!* And then you come along on a random Thursday, la-di-da, and say, *Oh, by the way, Egyptian gods are just one small part of the cosmic absurdity. We've also got the Greeks to worry about! Hooray!*'

Annabeth couldn't follow everything Sadie had said – a funeral god boyfriend? – but she had to admit that giggling about it was healthier than curling into a ball and sobbing.

'Okay,' she admitted. 'It all sounds a little crazy, but I guess it makes sense. My teacher Chiron . . . for years he's been telling me that ancient gods are immortal because they're part of the fabric of civilization. If Greek gods can stick around all these millennia, why not the Egyptians?'

'The more the merrier,' Sadie agreed. 'But, erm, what about this little doggie?' She picked up a tiny seashell and bounced it off the head of the Labrador monster, which snarled in irritation. 'One minute it's sitting on the table in our library – a harmless artefact, a stone fragment from some statue, we think. The next minute it comes to life and breaks out of Brooklyn House. It shreds our magical wards, ploughs through Felix's penguins and shrugs off my spells like they're nothing.'

'Penguins?' Annabeth shook her head. 'No. Forget I asked.'

She studied the dog creature as it strained against its bonds. Red Greek letters and hieroglyphs swirled around it as if trying to form new symbols – a message Annabeth could almost read.

'Will those ropes hold?' she asked. 'They look like they're weakening.'

'No worries,' Sadie assured her. 'Those ropes have held gods before. And not small gods, mind you. Extra-large ones.'

'Um, okay. So you said the dog was part of a statue. Any idea *what* statue?'

'None.' Sadie shrugged. 'Cleo, our librarian, was just researching that question when Fido here woke up.'

'But it has to be connected to the other monster – the wolf and the lion heads. I got the impression they'd just come to life, too. They'd fused together and weren't used to working as a team. They got on that train searching for something – probably this dog.'

Sadie fiddled with her silver pendant. 'A monster with three heads: a lion, a wolf and a dog. All sticking out of . . . what was that conical thing? A shell? A torch?'

Annabeth's head started to spin again. *A torch.*

She flashed on a distant memory – maybe a picture she'd seen in a book. She hadn't considered that the monster's cone might be something you could hold, something that belonged in a massive hand. But a torch wasn't right . . .

'It's a sceptre,' she realized. 'I don't remember which god held it, but the three-headed staff was his symbol. He was . . . Greek, I think, but he was also from somewhere in Egypt –'

'Alexandria,' Sadie guessed.

Annabeth stared at her. 'How do you know?'

'Well, granted, I'm not a history nut like my brother, but I *have* been to Alexandria. I recall something about it being the capital when the Greeks ruled Egypt. Alexander the Great, wasn't it?'

Annabeth nodded. 'That's right. Alexander conquered Egypt and, after he died, his general Ptolemy took over. He wanted the Egyptians to accept him as their pharaoh, so he mashed the Egyptian gods and Greek gods together and made up new ones.'

'Sounds messy,' Sadie said. 'I prefer my gods unmashed.'

'But there was one god in particular . . . I can't remember his name. The three-headed creature was at the top of his sceptre . . .'

'Rather large sceptre,' Sadie noted. 'I don't fancy meeting the bloke who could carry it around.'

'Oh, gods.' Annabeth sat up. 'That's it! The staff isn't just trying to reassemble itself – it's trying to find its master.'

Sadie scowled. 'I'm not in favour of that at all. We need to make sure –'

The dog monster howled. The magical ropes exploded like a grenade, spraying the beach with golden shrapnel.

*

The blast knocked Sadie across the dunes like tumbleweed.

Annabeth slammed into the ice-cream truck. Her limbs turned to lead. All the air was forced out of her lungs.

If the dog creature had wanted to kill her, it could have, easily.

Instead, it bounded inland, disappearing in the weeds.

Annabeth instinctively grabbed for a weapon. Her fingers closed round Sadie's curved wand. Pain made her gasp. The ivory burned like dry ice. Annabeth tried to let go, but her hand wouldn't obey. As she watched, the wand steamed, changing form until the burn subsided and Annabeth held a Celestial bronze dagger – just like the one she'd carried for years.

She stared at the blade. Then she heard groaning from the nearby dunes.

'Sadie!' Annabeth staggered to her feet.

By the time she reached the magician, Sadie was sitting up, spitting sand out of her mouth. She had bits of seaweed in her hair, and her backpack was wrapped round one of her combat boots, but she looked more outraged than injured.

'Stupid Fido!' she snarled. 'No dog biscuits for him!' She frowned at Annabeth's knife. 'Where did you get that?'

'Um . . . it's your wand,' Annabeth said. 'I picked it up and . . . I don't know. It just changed into the kind of dagger I usually use.'

'Huh. Well, magic items do have a mind of their own. Keep it. I've got more at home. Now, which way did Fido go?'

'Over there.' Annabeth pointed with her new blade.

Sadie peered inland. Her eyes widened. 'Oh . . . right. Towards the storm. That's new.'

Annabeth followed her gaze. Past the subway tracks, she saw nothing except an abandoned apartment tower, fenced off and forlorn against the late afternoon sky. 'What storm?'

'You don't see it?' Sadie asked. 'Hold on.' She disentangled her backpack from her boot and rummaged through her supplies. She brought out another ceramic vial, this one stubby and wide like a face-cream jar. She pulled off the lid and scooped out some pink goo. 'Let me smear this on your eyelids.'

'Wow, that sounds like an automatic *no*.'

'Don't be squeamish. It's perfectly harmless . . . well, for magicians. Probably for demigods, too.'

Annabeth wasn't reassured, but she closed her eyes. Sadie smeared on the gloop, which tingled and warmed like menthol rub.

'Right,' Sadie said. 'You can look now.'

Annabeth opened her eyes and gasped.

The world was awash in colour. The ground had turned translucent – gelatinous layers descending into darkness below. The air rippled with shimmering veils, each one vibrant but slightly out of sync, as if multiple high-definition videos had been superimposed on top of one another. Hieroglyphs and Greek letters swirled around her, fusing and bursting as they collided. Annabeth felt as if she were seeing the world on the atomic level. Everything invisible had been revealed, painted with magic light.

'Do – do you see like this all the time?'

Sadie snorted. 'Gods of Egypt, no! It would drive me bonkers. I have to concentrate to see the Duat. That's what you're doing – peering into the magical side of the world.'

'I . . .' Annabeth faltered.

Annabeth was usually a confident person. Whenever she dealt with regular mortals, she carried a smug certainty that she possessed secret knowledge. She understood the world of gods and monsters. Mortals didn't have a clue. Even with other demigods, Annabeth was almost always the most seasoned veteran. She'd done more than most heroes had ever dreamed of, and she'd survived.

Now, looking at the shifting curtains of colours, Annabeth felt like a six-year-old kid again, just learning how terrible and dangerous her world really was.

She sat down hard in the sand. 'I don't know what to think.'

'Don't think,' Sadie advised. 'Breathe. Your eyes will adjust. It's rather like swimming. If you let your body take over, you'll know what to do instinctively. Panic, and you'll drown.'

Annabeth tried to relax.

She began to discern patterns in the air: currents flowing between the layers of reality, vapour trails of magic streaming off cars and buildings. The site of the train wreck glowed green. Sadie had a golden aura with misty plumes spreading behind her like wings.

Where the dog monster once lay, the ground smouldered like live coals. Crimson tendrils snaked away from the site, following the direction in which the monster had fled.

Annabeth focused on the derelict apartment building in the distance, and her heartbeat doubled. The tower glowed red from the inside – light seeping through the boarded-up windows, shooting through cracks in the crumbling walls. Dark clouds swirled overhead, and more tendrils of red energy flowed towards the building from all over the landscape, as if being drawn into the vortex.

The scene reminded Annabeth of Charybdis, the whirlpool-inhaling monster she'd once encountered in the Sea of Monsters. It wasn't a happy memory.

'That apartment building,' she said. 'It's attracting red light from all over the place.'

'Exactly,' Sadie said. 'In Egyptian magic, red is bad. It means evil and chaos.'

'So that's where the dog monster is heading,' Annabeth guessed. 'To merge with the other piece of the sceptre –'

'And to find its master, I'd wager.'

Annabeth knew she should get up. They had to hurry. But, looking at the swirling layers of magic, she was afraid to move.

She'd spent her whole life learning about the Mist – the magical boundary that separated the mortal world from the world of Greek monsters and gods. But she'd never thought of the Mist as an actual curtain.

What had Sadie called it – the *Duat*?

Annabeth wondered if the Mist and the Duat were related, or maybe even the same thing. The number of veils she could see was overwhelming – like a tapestry folded in on itself a hundred times.

She didn't trust herself to stand. *Panic, and you'll drown.*

Sadie offered her hand. Her eyes were full of sympathy. 'Look, I know it's a lot, but nothing has changed. You're still the same tough-skinned, rucksack-wielding demigod you've always been. And now you have a lovely dagger as well.'

Annabeth felt the blood rise to her face. Normally she would've been the one giving the pep talk.

'Yeah. Yeah, of course.' She accepted Sadie's hand. 'Let's go find a god.'

A chain-link fence ringed the building, but they squeezed through a gap and picked their way across a field of spear grass and broken concrete.

The enchanted gloop on Annabeth's eyes seemed to be wearing off. The world no longer looked so multilayered and kaleidoscopic, but that was fine with her. She didn't need special vision to know the tower was full of bad magic.

Up close, the red glow in the windows was even more radiant. The plywood rattled. The brick walls groaned. Hieroglyphic birds and stick figures formed in the air and floated inside. Even the graffiti seemed to vibrate on the walls, as if the symbols were trying to come alive.

Whatever was inside the building, its power tugged at Annabeth too, the same way Crabby had on the train.

She gripped her new bronze dagger, realizing it was too small and too short to provide much offensive power. But that's why Annabeth *liked* daggers: they kept her focused. A child of Athena should never rely on a blade if she could use her wits instead. Intelligence won wars, not brute force.

Unfortunately, Annabeth's wits weren't working very well at the moment.

'Wish I knew what we were dealing with,' she muttered as they crept towards the building. 'I like to do research first – arm myself with knowledge.'

Sadie grunted. 'You sound like my brother. Tell me, how often do monsters give you the luxury of Googling them before they attack?'

'Never,' Annabeth admitted.

'Well, there you are. Carter – he would love to spend hours in the library, reading up on every hostile demon we might face, highlighting the important bits and making flash cards for me to study. Sadly, when demons attack, they don't give us any warning, and they rarely bother to identify themselves.'

'So what's *your* standard operating procedure?'

'Forge ahead,' Sadie said. 'Think on my feet. When necessary, blast enemies into teeny-tiny bits.'

'Great. You'd fit right in with my friends.'

'I'll take that as a compliment. That door, you think?'

A set of steps led to a basement entrance. A single two-by-four was nailed across the doorway in a half-hearted attempt to keep out trespassers, but the door itself was slightly ajar.

Annabeth was about to suggest scouting the perimeter. She didn't trust such an easy way in, but Sadie didn't wait. The young magician trotted down the steps and slipped inside.

Annabeth's only choice was to follow.

As it turned out, if they'd come through any other door, they would have died.

The whole interior of the building was a cavernous shell, thirty storeys tall, swirling with a maelstrom of bricks, pipes, boards and other debris, along with glowing Greek symbols, hieroglyphs and red neon tufts of energy. The scene was both terrifying and beautiful – as if a tornado had been caught, illuminated from within and put on permanent display.

Because they'd entered on the basement level, Sadie and Annabeth were protected in a shallow stairwell – a kind of trench in the concrete. If they'd walked into the storm on ground level, they would've been ripped to shreds.

As Annabeth watched, a twisted steel girder flew overhead at race-car speed. Dozens of bricks sped by like a school of fish. A fiery red hieroglyph slammed into a flying sheet of plywood, and the wood ignited like tissue paper.

'Up there,' Sadie whispered.

She pointed to the top of the building, where part of the thirtieth floor was still intact – a crumbling ledge jutting out into the void. It was hard to see through the swirling rubble and red haze, but Annabeth could discern a bulky humanoid shape standing at the precipice, his arms spread as if welcoming the storm.

'What's he doing?' Sadie murmured.

Annabeth flinched as a helix of copper pipes spun a few inches over her head. She stared into the debris and began noticing patterns like she had with the Duat: a swirl of boards and nails coming together to form a platform frame, a cluster of bricks assembling like Lego to make an arch.

'He's building something,' she realized.

'Building what, a disaster?' Sadie asked. 'This place reminds me of the Realm of Chaos. And, believe me, that was *not* my favourite holiday spot.'

Annabeth glanced over. She wondered if Chaos meant the same thing for Egyptians as it did for Greeks. Annabeth had had her own close call with Chaos, and if Sadie had been there, too . . . well, the magician must be even tougher than she seemed.

'The storm isn't completely random,' Annabeth said. 'See there? And there? Bits of material are coming together, forming some kind of structure inside the building.'

Sadie frowned. 'Looks like bricks in a blender to me.'

Annabeth wasn't sure how to explain it, but she'd studied architecture and engineering long enough to recognize the details. Copper piping was reconnecting like arteries and veins in a circulatory system. Sections of old walls were piecing themselves together to form a new jigsaw puzzle. Every so often, more bricks or girders peeled off the outer walls to join the tornado.

'He's cannibalizing the building,' she said. 'I don't know how long the outer walls will last.'

Sadie swore under her breath. 'Please tell me he's not building a pyramid. Anything but that.'

Annabeth wondered why an Egyptian magician would hate pyramids, but she shook her head. 'I'd guess it's some kind of conical tower. There's only one way to know for sure.'

'Ask the builder.' Sadie gazed up at the remnant of the thirtieth floor.

The man on the ledge hadn't moved, but Annabeth could swear he'd grown larger. Red light swirled around him. In silhouette, he looked like he was wearing a tall angular top hat *à la* Abe Lincoln.

Sadie shouldered her backpack. 'So, if that's our mystery god, where's the –'

Right on cue, a three-part howl cut through the din. At the opposite end of the building, a set of metal doors burst open and the crab monster loped inside.

Unfortunately, the beast now had all three heads – wolf, lion and dog. Its long spiral shell glowed with Greek and hieroglyphic inscriptions. Completely ignoring the flying debris, the monster clambered inside on its six forelegs, then leaped into the air. The storm carried it upward, spiralling through the chaos.

'It's heading for its master,' Annabeth said. 'We have to stop it.'

'Lovely,' Sadie grumbled. 'This is going to drain me.'

'What will?'

Sadie raised her staff. '*N'dah.*'

A golden hieroglyph blazed in the air above them:

And suddenly they were surrounded in a sphere of light.

Annabeth's spine tingled. She'd been encased in a protective bubble like this once before, when she, Percy and Grover had used magic pearls to escape the Underworld. The experience had been . . . claustrophobic.

'This will shield us from the storm?' she asked.

'Hopefully.' Sadie's face was now beaded with sweat. 'Come on.'

She led the way up the steps.

Immediately, their shield was put to the test. A flying kitchen counter would have decapitated them, but it shattered against Sadie's force field. Chunks of marble swirled harmlessly around them.

'Brilliant,' Sadie said. 'Now, hold the staff while I turn into a bird.'

'Wait. *What?*'

Sadie rolled her eyes. 'We're thinking on our feet, remember? I'll fly up there and stop the staff monster. You try to distract that god . . . whoever he is. Get his attention.'

'Fine, but I'm no magician. I can't maintain a spell.'

'The shield will hold for a few minutes, as long as you use the staff.'

'But what about you? If you're not inside the shield –'

'I have an idea. It might even work.'

Sadie fished something out of her pack – a small animal figurine. She curled her fingers round it, then began to change form.

Annabeth had seen people turn into animals before, but it never got easier to watch. Sadie shrank to a tenth of her size. Her nose elongated into a beak. Her hair and clothes and backpack melted into a sleek coat of feathers. She became a small bird of prey – a kite, maybe – her blue eyes now brilliant gold. With the little figurine still clutched in her talons, Sadie spread her wings and launched herself into the storm.

Annabeth winced as a cluster of bricks ploughed into her friend – but somehow the debris went straight through without turning Sadie into feather puree. Sadie's form just shimmered as if she were travelling under a deep layer of water.

Sadie was in the Duat, Annabeth realized – flying on a different level of reality.

The idea made Annabeth's mind heat up with possibilities. If a demigod could learn to pass through walls like that, run straight through monsters . . .

But that was a conversation for another time. Right now she needed to move. She charged up the steps and into the maelstrom. Metal bars and copper pipes clanged against her force field. The golden sphere flashed a little more dimly each time it deflected debris.

She raised Sadie's staff in one hand and her new dagger in the other. In the magical torrent, the Celestial bronze blade guttered like a dying torch.

'Hey!' she yelled at the ledge far above. 'Mr God Person!'

No response. Her voice probably couldn't carry over the storm.

The shell of the building started to groan. Mortar trickled from the walls and swirled into the mix like candy-floss tufts.

Sadie the hawk was still alive, flying towards the three-headed monster as it spiralled upward. The beast was about halfway to the top now, flailing its legs and glowing ever more brightly, as if soaking up the power of the tornado.

Annabeth was running out of time.

She reached into her memory, sifting through old myths, the most obscure tales Chiron had ever told her at camp. When she was younger, she'd been like a sponge, soaking up every fact and name.

The three-headed staff. The god of Alexandria, Egypt.

The god's name came to her. At least, she hoped she was right.

One of the first lessons she'd learned as a demigod: *Names have power*. You never said the name of a god or monster unless you were prepared to draw its attention.

Annabeth took a deep breath. She shouted at the top of her lungs: 'SERAPIS!'

The storm slowed. Huge sections of pipe hovered in midair. Clouds of bricks and timber froze and hung suspended.

Becalmed in the middle of the tornado, the three-headed monster tried to stand. Sadie swooped overhead, opened her talons and dropped her figurine, which instantly grew into a full-sized camel.

The shaggy dromedary slammed into the monster's back. Both creatures tumbled out of the air and crashed to the floor in a tangle of limbs and heads. The staff monster continued to struggle, but the camel lay on top of it with its legs splayed, bleating and spitting and basically going limp like a thousand-pound toddler throwing a tantrum.

From the thirtieth-floor ledge, a man's voice boomed: 'WHO DARES INTERRUPT MY TRIUMPHAL RISE?'

'I do!' yelled Annabeth. 'Come down and face me!'

She didn't like taking credit for other people's camels, but she wanted to keep the god focused on her so Sadie could do . . . whatever Sadie decided to do. The young magician clearly had some good tricks up her sleeve.

The god Serapis leaped from his ledge. He plummeted thirty storeys and landed on his feet in the middle of the ground floor, an easy dagger throw away from Annabeth.

Not that she was tempted to attack.

Serapis stood fifteen feet tall. He wore only a pair of swimming trunks in a Hawaiian floral pattern. His body rippled with muscles. His bronze skin was covered in shimmering tattoos of hieroglyphs, Greek letters and other languages Annabeth didn't recognize.

His face was framed with long, frizzy braided hair like Rastafarian dreadlocks. A curly Greek beard grew down to his collarbone. His eyes were sea green – so much like Percy's that Annabeth got goosebumps.

Normally she didn't like hairy bearded dudes, but she had

to admit this god was attractive in an older, wild-surfer kind of way.

His headgear, however, ruined the look. What Annabeth had taken for a stovepipe hat was actually a cylindrical wicker basket embroidered with images of pansies.

'Excuse me,' she said. 'Is that a flowerpot on your head?'

Serapis raised his bushy brown eyebrows. He patted his head as if he'd forgotten about the basket. A few wheat seeds spilled from the top. 'That's a *modius,* silly girl. It's one of my holy symbols! The grain basket represents the Underworld, which I control.'

'Uh, you do?'

'Of course!' Serapis glowered. 'Or I *did,* and soon I will again. But who are you to criticize my fashion choices? A Greek demigod, by the smell of you, carrying a Celestial bronze weapon and an Egyptian staff from the House of Life. Which are you – hero or magician?'

Annabeth's hands trembled. Flowerpot hat or no, Serapis radiated power. Standing so near him, Annabeth felt watery inside, as if her heart, her stomach and her courage were all melting.

Get a hold of yourself, she thought. *You've met plenty of gods before.*

But Serapis was different. His presence felt fundamentally *wrong* – as if simply by being here he was pulling Annabeth's world inside out.

Twenty feet behind the god, Sadie the bird landed and changed back to human form. She gestured to Annabeth: finger to lips (*shh*), then rolled her hand (*keep him talking*). She began rooting quietly through her bag.

Annabeth had no idea what her friend was planning, but she forced herself to meet Serapis's eyes. 'Who says I'm not both – magician *and* demigod? Now, explain why you're here!'

Serapis's face darkened. Then, to Annabeth's surprise, he threw back his head and laughed, spilling more grain from his *modius*. 'I see! Trying to impress me, eh? You think yourself worthy of being my high priestess?'

Annabeth gulped. There was only one answer to a question like that. 'Of course I'm worthy! Why, I was once the *magna mater* of Athena's cult! But are you worthy of my service?'

'HA!' Serapis grinned. 'A big mother of Athena's cult, eh? Let's see how tough you are.'

He flicked his hand. A bathtub flew out of the air, straight at Annabeth's force field. The porcelain burst into shrapnel against the golden sphere, but Sadie's staff became so hot that Annabeth had to drop it. The white wood burned to ashes.

Great, she thought. *Two minutes, and I've already ruined Sadie's staff.*

Her protective shield was gone. She faced a fifteen-foot-tall god with only her usual weapons – a tiny dagger and a lot of attitude.

To Annabeth's left, the three-headed monster was still struggling to get out from under the camel, but the camel was heavy, stubborn and fabulously uncoordinated. Every time the monster tried to push it off, the camel farted with gusto and splayed its legs even further.

Meanwhile, Sadie had taken a piece of chalk from her bag. She scribbled furiously on the concrete floor behind Serapis, perhaps writing a nice epitaph to commemorate their imminent death.

Annabeth recalled a quote her friend Frank had once shared with her – something from Sun Tzu's *The Art of War.*

When weak, act strong.

Annabeth stood straight and laughed in Serapis's face. 'Throw things at me all you want, Lord Serapis. I don't even need a staff to defend myself. My powers are too great! Or perhaps you want to stop wasting my time and tell me how I may serve you, *assuming* I agree to become your new high priestess.'

The god's face glowed with outrage.

Annabeth was sure he would drop the entire whirlwind of debris on her, and there was no way she'd be able to stop it. She considered throwing her dagger at the god's eye, the way her friend Rachel had once distracted the Titan Kronos, but Annabeth didn't trust her aim.

Finally Serapis gave her a twisted smile. 'You have courage, girl. I'll grant you that. And you did make haste to find me. Perhaps you *can* serve. You will be the first of many to give me your power, your life, your very soul!'

'Sounds fun.' Annabeth glanced at Sadie, wishing she would hurry up with that chalk art.

'But first,' Serapis said, 'I must have my staff!'

He gestured towards the camel. A red hieroglyph burned on the creature's hide, and, with one final fart, the poor dromedary dissolved into a pile of sand.

The three-headed monster got to its forepaws, shaking off the sand.

'Hold it!' Annabeth yelled.

The monster's three heads snarled at her.

Serapis scowled. 'What now, girl?'

'Well, I should . . . you know, present the staff to you, as your high priestess! We should do things properly!'

Annabeth lunged for the monster. It was much too heavy for her to pick up, but she stuck her dagger in her belt and used both hands to grab the end of the creature's conical shell, dragging it backwards, away from the god.

Meanwhile, Sadie had drawn a big circle about the size of a hula-hoop on the concrete. She was now decorating it with hieroglyphs, using several different colours of chalk.

By all means, Annabeth thought with frustration. *Take your time and make it pretty!*

She managed to smile at Serapis while holding back the staff monster that was still trying to claw its way forward.

'Now, my lord,' Annabeth said, 'tell me your glorious plan! Something about souls and lives?'

The staff monster howled in protest, probably because it could see Sadie hiding behind the god, doing her top-secret pavement art. Serapis didn't seem to notice.

'Behold!' He spread his muscular arms. 'The new centre of my power!'

Red sparks blazed through the frozen whirlwind. A web of light connected the dots until Annabeth saw the glowing outline of the structure Serapis was building: a massive tower three hundred feet tall, designed in three tapering tiers – a square bottom, an octagonal middle and a circular top. At the zenith blazed a fire as bright as a Cyclops's forge.

'A lighthouse,' Annabeth said. 'The Lighthouse of Alexandria.'

'Indeed, my young priestess.' Serapis paced back and forth like a teacher giving a lecture, though his floral-print shorts were pretty distracting. His wicker-basket hat kept tilting to one side or the other, spilling grain. Somehow he still failed to notice Sadie squatting behind him, scribbling pretty pictures with her chalk.

'Alexandria!' the god cried. 'Once the greatest city in the world, the ultimate fusion of Greek and Egyptian power! I was its supreme god, and now I have risen again. I will create my new capital here!'

'Uh . . . in Rockaway Beach?'

Serapis stopped and scratched his beard. 'You have a point. That name won't do. We will call it . . . Rockandria? Serapaway? Well, we'll figure that out later! Our first step is to complete my new lighthouse. It will be a beacon to the world – drawing the deities of Ancient Greece and Egypt here to me just as it did in the old days. I shall feed on their essence and become the most powerful god of all!'

Annabeth felt as if she'd swallowed a tablespoon of salt. '*Feed on their essence.* You mean, destroy them?'

Serapis waved dismissively. '*Destroy* is such an ugly word. I prefer *incorporate*. You know my history, I hope? When Alexander the Great conquered Egypt –'

'He tried to merge the Greek and Egyptian religions,' Annabeth said.

'Tried and failed.' Serapis chuckled. 'Alexander chose an Egyptian sun god, Amun, to be his main deity. That didn't work too well. The Greeks didn't like Amun. Neither did the Egyptians of the Nile Delta. They saw Amun as an upriver god. But when Alexander died his general took over Egypt.'

'Ptolemy the First,' Annabeth said.

Serapis beamed, obviously pleased. 'Yes . . . Ptolemy. Now, there was a mortal with *vision!*'

It took all of Annabeth's will not to stare at Sadie, who had now completed her magic circle and was tapping the hieroglyphs with her finger, muttering something under her breath as if to activate them.

The three-headed staff monster snarled in disapproval. It tried to lunge forward, and Annabeth barely managed to hold him back. Her fingers were weakening. The creature's aura was as nauseating as ever.

'Ptolemy created a new god,' she said, straining with effort. 'He created you.'

Serapis shrugged. 'Well, not from *scratch*. I was once a minor village god. Nobody had even heard of me! But Ptolemy discovered my statue and brought it to Alexandria. He had the Greek and Egyptian priests do auguries and incantations and whatnot. They all agreed that I was the great god Serapis, and I should be worshipped above all other gods. I was an instant hit!'

Sadie rose within her magic circle. She unlatched her silver necklace and began swinging it like a lasso.

The three-headed monster roared what was probably a warning to its master: *Look out!*

But Serapis was on a roll. As he spoke, the hieroglyphic and Greek tattoos on his skin glowed more brightly.

'I became the most important god of the Greeks and Egyptians!' he said. 'As more people worshipped me, I drained the power of the older gods. Slowly but surely, I took their place. The Underworld? I became its master, replacing both Hades and Osiris. The guard dog Cerberus transformed into my staff, which you now hold. His three heads represent the past, present and future – all of which I will control when the staff is returned to my grasp.'

The god held out his hand. The monster strained to reach him. Annabeth's arm muscles burned. Her fingers began to slip.

Sadie was still swinging her pendant, muttering an incantation.

Holy Hecate, Annabeth thought, *how long does it take to cast a stupid spell?*

She caught Sadie's gaze and saw the message in her eyes: *Hold on. Just another few seconds.*

Annabeth wasn't sure she had a few more seconds.

'The Ptolemaic dynasty . . .' She gritted her teeth. 'It fell centuries ago. Your cult was forgotten. How is it that you're back now?'

Serapis sniffed. 'That's not important. The one who awakened me . . . well, he has delusions of grandeur. He thinks he can control me just because he found some old spells in the Book of Thoth.'

Behind the god, Sadie flinched as if she'd been smacked between the eyes. Apparently, this 'Book of Thoth' struck a chord with her.

'You see,' Serapis continued, 'back in the day, King Ptolemy decided it wasn't enough to make *me* a major god. He wanted to become immortal, too. He declared himself a god, but his magic backfired. After his death, his family was cursed for generations. The Ptolemaic line grew weaker and weaker until that silly girl Cleopatra committed suicide and gave everything to the Romans.'

The god sneered. 'Mortals . . . always so greedy. The magician who awakened me *this* time thinks he can do better than Ptolemy. Raising me was only one of his experiments with hybrid Greek-Egyptian magic. He wishes to make himself a god, but he has overstepped himself. I am awake now. *I* will control the universe.'

Serapis fixed Annabeth with his brilliant green eyes. His features seemed to shift, reminding Annabeth of many different Olympians: Zeus, Poseidon, Hades. Something about his smile even reminded Annabeth of her mother, Athena.

'Just think, little demigod,' Serapis said, 'this lighthouse will draw the gods to me like moths to a candle. Once I have consumed their power, I will raise a great city. I will build a new Alexandrian library with all the knowledge of the ancient world, both Greek and Egyptian. As a child of Athena, you should appreciate this. As my high priestess, think of all the power you will have!'

A new Alexandrian library.

Annabeth couldn't pretend that the idea didn't thrill her. So much knowledge of the ancient world had been destroyed when that library had burned.

Serapis must have seen the hunger in her eyes.

'Yes.' He extended his hand. 'Enough talk, girl. Give me my staff!'

'You're right,' Annabeth croaked. 'Enough talk.'

She drew her dagger and plunged it into the monster's shell.

So many things could have gone wrong. Most of them did.

Annabeth was hoping the knife would split the shell, maybe even destroy the monster. Instead, it opened a tiny fissure that spewed red magic as hot as a line of magma. Annabeth stumbled back, her eyes stinging.

Serapis bellowed, 'TREACHERY!' The staff creature howled and thrashed, its three heads trying in vain to reach the knife stuck in its back.

At the same moment, Sadie cast her spell. She threw her silver necklace and yelled, '*Tyet!*'

The pendant exploded. A giant silvery hieroglyph enveloped the god like a see-through coffin:

Serapis roared as his arms were pinned to his side.

Sadie shouted, 'I name you Serapis, god of Alexandria! God of . . . uh, funny hats and three-headed staffs! I bind you with the power of Isis!'

Debris began falling out of the air, crashing around Annabeth. She dodged a brick wall and a fuse box. Then she noticed the wounded staff monster crawling towards Serapis.

She lunged in that direction, only to get smacked in the head by a falling piece of timber. She hit the floor hard, her skull throbbing, and was immediately buried in more debris.

She took a shaky breath. 'Ow, ow, ow.'

At least she hadn't been buried in bricks. She kicked her way out of a pile of plywood and plucked a six-inch splinter out of her shirt.

The monster had made it to Serapis's feet. Annabeth knew she should have stabbed one of the monster's heads, but she just couldn't make herself do it. She was always a softie when it came to animals, even if they were part of a magical evil creature trying to kill her. Now it was too late.

The god flexed his considerable muscles. The silvery prison shattered around him. The three-headed staff flew into his hand, and Serapis turned on Sadie Kane.

Her protective circle evaporated in a cloud of red steam.

'You would *bind* me?' Serapis cried. 'You would *name* me? You do not even have the proper language to name me, little magician!'

Annabeth staggered forward, but her breathing was shallow. Now that Serapis held the staff, his aura felt ten times more powerful. Annabeth's ears buzzed. Her ankles turned to mush. She could feel her life force being drained away – vacuumed into the red halo of the god.

Somehow, Sadie stood her ground, her expression defiant. 'Right, Lord Cereal Bowl. You want proper language? *HA-DI!*'

A new hieroglyph blazed in Serapis's face:

But the god swiped it out of the air with his free hand. He closed his fist and smoke shot between his fingers, as if he'd just crushed a miniature steam engine.

Sadie gulped. 'That's impossible. How –'

'Expecting an explosion?' Serapis laughed. 'Sorry to disappoint you, child, but my power is both Greek and

Egyptian. It combines both, consumes both, *replaces* both. You are favoured of Isis, I see? Excellent. She was once my wife.'

'*What?*' Sadie cried. 'No. No, no, no.'

'Oh, yes! When I deposed both Osiris and Zeus, Isis was forced to serve me. Now I will use you as a gateway to summon her here and bind her. Isis will once again be my queen!'

Serapis thrust out his staff. From each of the three monstrous mouths, red tendrils of light shot forth, encircling Sadie like thorny branches.

Sadie screamed, and Annabeth finally overcame her shock.

She grabbed the nearest sheet of plywood – a wobbly square about the size of a shield – and tried to remember her Ultimate Frisbee lessons from Camp Half-Blood.

'Hey, Grain Head!' she yelled.

She twisted from the waist, using the force of her entire body. The plywood sailed through the air just as Serapis turned to look at her, and the edge smacked him between the eyes.

'GAH!'

Annabeth dived to one side as Serapis blindly thrust his staff in her direction. The three monster heads blasted superheated plumes of vapour, melting a hole in the concrete where Annabeth had just been standing.

She kept moving, picking her way through mounds of debris that now littered the floor. She dived behind a pile of broken toilets as the god's staff blasted another triple column of steam in her direction, coming so close that she felt blisters rise on the back of her neck.

Annabeth spotted Sadie about thirty yards away, on her feet and staggering away from Serapis. At least she was still alive. But Annabeth knew she would need time to recover.

'Hey, Serapis!' Annabeth called from behind the mountain of commodes. 'How did that plywood taste?'

'Child of Athena!' the god bellowed. 'I will devour your life force! I will use you to destroy your wretched mother! You think you are wise? You are nothing compared to the one who awakened me, and even *he* does not understand the power he has unleashed. None of you shall gain the crown of immortality. I control the past, present and future. I alone will rule the gods!'

And thank you for the long speech, Annabeth thought.

By the time Serapis blasted her position, turning the toilets into a porcelain slag heap, Annabeth had crept halfway across the room.

She was searching for Sadie when the magician popped up from her hiding place, only ten feet away, and shouted: '*Suh–FAH!*'

Annabeth turned as a new hieroglyph, twenty feet tall, blazed on the wall behind Serapis:

Mortar disintegrated. The side of the building groaned, and as Serapis screamed, 'NO!' the entire wall collapsed on top of him in a brick tidal wave, burying him under a thousand tons of wreckage.

Annabeth choked on a cloud of dust. Her eyes stung. She felt as if she'd been parboiled in a rice cooker, but she stumbled to Sadie's side.

The young magician was covered in lime powder as if she'd been rolled in sugar. She stared at the gaping hole she'd made in the side of the building.

'That worked,' she muttered.

'It was genius.' Annabeth squeezed her shoulders. 'What spell was that?'

'*Loosen*,' Sadie said. 'I reckoned . . . well, making things fall apart is usually easier than putting them together.'

As if in agreement, the remaining shell of the building creaked and rumbled.

'Come on.' Annabeth took Sadie's hand. 'We need to get out of here. These walls –'

The foundations shook. From beneath the rubble came a muffled roar. Shafts of red light shot from gaps in the debris.

'Oh, please!' Sadie protested. 'He's still *alive*?'

Annabeth's heart sank, but she wasn't surprised. 'He's a god. He's immortal.'

'Well, then how –?'

Serapis's hand, still clutching his staff, thrust through the bricks and boards. The monster's three heads blasted shafts of steam in all directions. Annabeth's knife remained hilt-deep in the monster's shell, the scar round it venting red-hot hieroglyphs, Greek letters and English curse words – thousands of years of bad language spilling free.

Like a time line, Annabeth thought.

Suddenly an idea clicked in her mind. 'Past, present and future. He controls them all.'

'What?' Sadie asked.

'The staff is the key,' Annabeth said. 'We have to destroy it.'

'Yes, but –'

Annabeth sprinted towards the pile of rubble. Her eyes were fixed on the hilt of her dagger, but she was too late.

Serapis's other arm broke free, then his head, his flower-basket hat crushed and leaking grain. Annabeth's plywood Frisbee had broken his nose and blackened his eyes, leaving a mask like a raccoon's.

'Kill you!' he bellowed, just as Sadie yelled an encore: '*Suh–FAH!*'

Annabeth beat a hasty retreat, and Serapis screamed, 'NO!' as another thirty-storey section of wall collapsed on top of him.

The magic must have been too much for Sadie. She crumpled like a rag doll, and Annabeth caught her just before her head hit the ground. As the remaining sections of wall shuddered and leaned inward, Annabeth scooped up the younger girl and carried her outside.

Somehow she cleared the building before the rest of it collapsed. Annabeth heard the tremendous roar, but she wasn't sure if it was the devastation behind her or the sound of her own skull splitting from pain and exhaustion.

She staggered on until she reached the subway tracks. She set Sadie down gently in the weeds.

Sadie's eyes rolled back in her head. She muttered incoherently. Her skin felt so feverish that Annabeth had to fight down a sense of panic. Steam rose from the magician's sleeves.

Over by the train wreck, the mortals had noticed the new disaster. Emergency vehicles were peeling away, heading for the collapsed apartment building. A news helicopter circled overhead.

Annabeth was tempted to yell for medical help, but, before she could, Sadie inhaled sharply. Her eyelids fluttered.

She spat a chip of concrete out of her mouth, sat up weakly and stared at the column of dust churning into the sky from their little adventure.

'Right,' Sadie muttered. 'What should we destroy next?'

Annabeth sobbed with relief. 'Thank the gods you're okay. You were literally steaming.'

'Hazard of the trade.' Sadie brushed some dust off her face. 'Too much magic and I can literally burn up. That's about as close to self-immolation as I'd like to come today.'

Annabeth nodded. She'd been jealous of all those cool spells Sadie could cast, but now she was glad to be just a demigod. 'No more magic for you.'

'Not for a while.' Sadie grimaced. 'I don't suppose Serapis is defeated?'

Annabeth gazed towards the site of the would-be lighthouse. She wanted to think the god was gone, but she knew better. She could still feel his aura disrupting the world, pulling at her soul and draining her energy.

'We've got a few minutes at best,' she guessed. 'He'll work his way free. Then he'll come after us.'

Sadie groaned. 'We need reinforcements. Sadly, I don't have enough energy to open a portal, even if I could find one. Isis isn't responding to me, either. She knows better than to show up and have her essence absorbed by Lord Cereal Bowl.' She sighed. 'I don't suppose you have any other demigods on speed dial?'

'If only . . .' Annabeth faltered.

She realized her own backpack was still on her shoulder. How had it not slipped off during the fight? And why did it feel so light?

She unslung the pack and opened the top. The architecture books were gone. Instead, nestled at the bottom was a brownie-sized square of ambrosia wrapped in cellophane, and under that . . .

Annabeth's lower lip trembled. She pulled out something she hadn't carried with her in a long time: her battered blue New York Yankees cap.

She glanced up at the darkening sky. 'Mom?'

No reply, but Annabeth couldn't think of any other explanation. Her mother had sent her help. The realization both encouraged and terrified her. If Athena was taking a personal interest in this situation, Serapis truly was a monumental threat – not just to Annabeth but to the gods.

'It's a baseball cap,' Sadie noted. 'Is that good?'

'I – I think so,' Annabeth said. 'The last time I wore it, the magic didn't work. But if it *does* . . . I might have a plan. It'll be your turn to keep Serapis distracted.'

Sadie frowned. 'Did I mention I'm out of magic?'

'That's okay,' Annabeth said. 'How are you at bluffing, lying and trash-talking?'

Sadie raised an eyebrow. 'I've been told those are my most attractive qualities.'

'Excellent,' Annabeth said. 'Then it's time I taught you some Greek.'

They didn't have long.

Annabeth had barely finished coaching Sadie when the ruined building shook, debris exploded outwards, and Serapis emerged, roaring and cursing.

Startled emergency workers scattered from the scene, but

they didn't seem to notice the fifteen-foot-tall god marching away from the wreckage, his three-headed staff spewing steam and red beams of magic into the sky.

Serapis headed straight in Sadie and Annabeth's direction.

'Ready?' Annabeth asked.

Sadie exhaled. 'Do I have a choice?'

'Here.' Annabeth gave her the square of ambrosia. 'Demigod food. It might restore your strength.'

'*Might*, eh?'

'If I can use your healing potion, you should be able to eat ambrosia.'

'Cheers, then.' Sadie took a bite. Colour returned to her cheeks. Her eyes brightened. 'Tastes like my gran's scones.'

Annabeth smiled. 'Ambrosia always tastes like your favourite comfort food.'

'That's a shame.' Sadie took another bite and swallowed. 'Gran's scones are always burnt and rather horrid. Ah – here comes our friend.'

Serapis kicked a fire engine out of his way and lumbered towards the train tracks. He didn't seem to have spotted Sadie and Annabeth yet, but Annabeth guessed he could *sense* them. He scanned the horizon, his expression full of murderous rage.

'Here we go.' Annabeth donned her Yankees cap.

Sadie's eyes widened. 'Well done. You're quite invisible. You won't start shooting sparks, will you?'

'Why would I do that?'

'Oh . . . my brother cast an invisibility spell once. Didn't work out so well. Anyway, good luck.'

'You, too.'

Annabeth dashed to one side as Sadie waved her arms and yelled, 'Oi, Serapis!'

'DEATH TO YOU!' the god bellowed.

He barrelled forward, his massive feet making craters in the tarmac.

As they'd planned, Sadie backed towards the beach. Annabeth crouched behind an abandoned car and waited for Serapis to pass. Invisible or not, she wasn't going to take any chances.

'Come on!' Sadie taunted the god. 'Is that the fastest you can run, you overgrown village idiot?'

'RAR!' The god charged past Annabeth's position.

She ran after Serapis, who caught up with Sadie at the edge of the surf.

The god raised his glowing staff, all three monstrous heads belching steam. 'Any last words, magician?'

'For you? Yes!' Sadie whirled her arms in movements that could've been magic – or possibly kung fu.

'*Meana aedei thea!*' She chanted the lines Annabeth had taught her. '*En . . . ponte pathen algae!*'

Annabeth winced. Sadie's pronunciation was pretty bad. She'd got the first line right, more or less: *Sing of rage, O goddess.* But the second line should've been: *In the sea, suffer misery.* Instead, Sadie had said something like: *In the sea, suffer moss!*

Fortunately, the sound of Ancient Greek was enough to shock Serapis. The god wavered, his three-headed staff still raised. 'What are you –'

'Isis, hear me!' Sadie continued. 'Athena, to my aid!' She rattled off some more phrases – some Greek, some Ancient Egyptian.

Meanwhile, Annabeth sneaked up behind the god, her eyes on the dagger still impaled in the monster's shell. If Serapis would just lower his staff . . .

'*Alpha, beta, gamma!*' Sadie cried. '*Gyros, spanakopita. Presto!*' She beamed in triumph. 'There. You're done for!'

Serapis stared at her, clearly baffled. The red tattoos on his skin dimmed. A few of the symbols turned into question marks and sad faces. Annabeth crept closer . . . twenty feet from him now.

'Done for?' Serapis asked. 'What on earth are you talking about, girl? I'm about to destroy you.'

'And if you do,' Sadie warned, 'you will activate the death link that sends you to oblivion!'

'Death link? There is no such thing!' Serapis lowered his staff. The three animal heads were level with Annabeth's eyes.

Her heart pounded. Ten feet to go. Then, if she jumped, she might be able to reach the dagger. She'd only have one chance to pull it out.

The heads of the staff didn't seem to notice her. They snarled and snapped, spitting steam in random directions. Wolf, lion, dog – past, present and future.

To do maximum damage, she knew which head she had to strike.

But why did the future have to be a dog? That black Labrador was the least threatening of the monster heads. With its big gold eyes and floppy ears, it reminded Annabeth of too many friendly pets she'd known.

It's not a real animal, she told herself. *It's part of a magical staff.*

But, as she got within striking distance, her arms grew heavy. She couldn't look at the dog without feeling guilty.

The future is a good thing, the dog seemed to say. *It's cute and fuzzy!*

If Annabeth struck at the Labrador's head, what if she killed her *own* future – the plans she had for college, the plans she'd made with Percy . . . ?

Sadie was still talking. Her tone had taken on a harder edge.

'My mother, Ruby Kane,' Sadie told Serapis, 'she gave her life to seal Apophis in the Duat. *Apophis*, mind you – who is thousands of years older than you and much more powerful. So if you think I'm going to let a second-rate god take over the world, think again!'

The anger in her voice was no mere bluff, and suddenly Annabeth was glad she'd given Sadie the job of facing down Serapis. The magician was surprisingly terrifying when she wanted to be.

Serapis shifted his weight uneasily. 'I will destroy you!'

'Good luck,' Sadie said. 'I've bound you with Greek and Egyptian spells so powerful they will scatter your atoms to the stars.'

'You lie!' Serapis yelled. 'I feel no spell upon me. Even the one who summoned me had no such magic.'

Annabeth was face to face with the black dog. The dagger

was just overhead, but every molecule in her body rebelled at the idea of killing the animal . . . killing the future.

Meanwhile, Sadie managed a brave laugh. 'The one who summoned you? You mean that old con artist Setne?'

Annabeth didn't know the name, but Serapis obviously did. The air around him rippled with heat. The lion snarled. The wolf bared its teeth.

'Oh, yes,' Sadie continued. 'I'm very familiar with Setne. I suppose he didn't tell you who let him back into the world. He's only alive because *I* spared him. You think *his* magic is powerful? Try me. Do it NOW.'

Annabeth stirred. She realized Sadie was talking to *her*, not the god. The bluff was getting old. She was out of time.

Serapis sneered. 'Nice try, magician.'

As he raised his staff to strike, Annabeth jumped. Her hand closed round the hilt of the dagger, and she pulled it free.

'What?' Serapis cried.

Annabeth let loose a guttural sob and plunged her dagger into the dog's neck.

She expected an explosion.

Instead, the dagger was sucked into the dog's neck like a

paper clip into a vacuum cleaner. Annabeth barely had time to let go.

She rolled free as the dog howled, shrinking and shrivelling until it imploded into the monster's shell. Serapis roared. He shook his sceptre but he couldn't seem to let go of it.

'What have you done?' he cried.

'Taken your future,' Annabeth said. 'Without that, you're nothing.'

The staff cracked open. It grew so hot that Annabeth felt the hairs on her arms start to burn. She crawled backwards through the sand as the lion and wolf heads were sucked into the shell. The entire staff collapsed into a red fireball in the god's palm.

Serapis tried to shake it off. It only glowed brighter. His fingers curled inward. His hand was consumed. His entire arm contracted and vaporized as it was drawn into the fiery sphere.

'I cannot be destroyed!' Serapis yelled. 'I am the pinnacle of your worlds combined! Without my guidance, you will never attain the crown! You all shall perish! You shall –'

The fireball flared and sucked the god into its vortex. Then it winked out as if it had never existed.

*

'Ugh,' Sadie said.

They sat on the beach at sunset, watching the tide and listening to the wail of emergency vehicles behind them.

Poor Rockaway. First a hurricane. Then a train wreck, a building collapse and a rampaging god all in one day. Some communities never catch a break.

Annabeth sipped her Ribena – a British drink that Sadie had summoned from her 'personal storage area' in the Duat.

'Don't worry,' Sadie assured her. 'Summoning snacks isn't hard magic.'

As thirsty as Annabeth was, the Ribena tasted even better than nectar.

Sadie seemed to be on the mend. The ambrosia had done its work. Now, rather than looking as if she was at death's door, she merely looked as if she'd been run over by a pack of mules.

The waves lapped at Annabeth's feet, helping her relax, but still she felt a residual disquiet from her encounter with Serapis – a humming in her body, as if all her bones had become tuning forks.

'You mentioned a name,' she recalled. 'Setne?'

Sadie wrinkled her nose. 'Long story. Evil magician, back from the dead.'

'Oh, I hate it when evil people come back from the dead. You said . . . you allowed him to go free?'

'Well, my brother and I needed his help. At the time, we didn't have much choice. At any rate, Setne escaped with the Book of Thoth, the most dangerous collection of spells in the world.'

'And Setne used that magic to awaken Serapis.'

'Stands to reason.' Sadie shrugged. 'The crocodile monster my brother and your boyfriend fought a while ago, the Son of Sobek . . . I wouldn't be surprised if that was another of Setne's experiments. He's trying to combine Greek and Egyptian magic.'

After the day she'd just had, Annabeth wanted to put her invisibility cap back on, crawl into a hole and sleep forever. She'd saved the world enough times already. She didn't want to think about another potential threat. Yet she couldn't ignore it. She fingered the brim of her Yankees cap and thought about why her mother had given it back to her today – its magic restored.

Athena seemed to be sending a message: *There will always be threats too powerful to face head-on. You are not done with stealth. You must tread carefully here.*

'Setne wants to be a god,' Annabeth said.

The wind off the water suddenly turned cold. It smelled less like fresh sea air, more like burning ruins.

'A god . . .' Sadie shuddered. 'That scrawny old codger with the loincloth and Elvis hair. What a horrible thought.'

Annabeth tried to picture the guy Sadie was describing. Then she decided she didn't want to.

'If Setne's goal is immortality,' Annabeth said, 'waking Serapis won't be his last trick.'

Sadie laughed without humour. 'Oh, no. He's only playing with us now. The Son of Sobek . . . Serapis. I'd wager that Setne planned both events just to see what would happen, how the demigods and magicians would react. He's testing his new magic, and our capabilities, before he makes his real bid for power.'

'He can't succeed,' Annabeth said hopefully. 'No one can make themselves a god just by casting a spell.'

Sadie's expression wasn't reassuring. 'I hope you're right. Because a god who knows both Greek and Egyptian magic, who can control both worlds . . . I can't even imagine.'

Annabeth's stomach twisted as if it were learning a new yoga position. In any war, good planning was more important than sheer power. If this Setne had orchestrated Percy and Carter's battle with that crocodile, if he'd engineered Serapis's rise so Sadie and Annabeth would be drawn to confront him . . . An enemy who planned so well would be very hard to stop.

She dug her toes into the sand. 'Serapis said something else before he disappeared – *you will never attain the crown*. I thought he meant it like a metaphor. Then I remembered what he said about Ptolemy I, the king who tried to become a god –'

'The crown of immortality,' Sadie recalled. 'Maybe a *pschent*.'

Annabeth frowned. 'I don't know that word. A *shent*?'

Sadie spelled it. 'An Egyptian crown, looks rather like a bowling pin. Not a lovely fashion statement, but the *pschent* invested the pharaoh with his divine power. If Setne is trying to recreate the old king's god-making magic, I bet five quid and a plate of Gran's burnt scones that he's trying to find the crown of Ptolemy.'

Annabeth decided not to take that bet. 'We have to stop him.'

'Right.' Sadie sipped her Ribena. 'I'll go back to Brooklyn House. After I smack my brother for not confiding in me about you demigod types, I'll put our researchers to work and see what we can learn about Ptolemy. Perhaps his crown is sitting in a museum somewhere.' Sadie curled her lip. 'Though I *do* hate museums.'

Annabeth traced her finger through the sand. Without really thinking about it, she drew the hieroglyphic symbol for Isis: the *tyet*. 'I'll do some research, too. My friends in the Hecate cabin may know something about Ptolemy's magic. Maybe I can get my mom to advise me.'

Thinking about her mother made her uneasy.

Today, Serapis had been on the verge of destroying both Annabeth and Sadie. He'd threatened to use them as gateways to draw Athena and Isis to their doom.

Sadie's eyes were stormy, as if she were thinking the same thoughts. 'We can't let Setne keep experimenting. He'll rip our worlds apart. We have to find this crown, or –'

She glanced into the sky and her voice faltered. 'Ah, my ride is here.'

Annabeth turned. For a moment she thought the *Argo II* was descending from the clouds, but this was a different kind of flying boat – a smaller Egyptian reed barque with painted eyes on the prow and a single white sail emblazoned with the *tyet* symbol.

It settled gently at the edge of the surf.

Sadie rose and brushed the sand off her trousers. 'Give you a lift home?'

Annabeth tried to imagine a boat like this sailing into

Camp Half-Blood. 'Um, it's okay. I can make it back.'

'Suit yourself.' Sadie shouldered her pack, then helped Annabeth up. 'You say Carter drew a hieroglyph on your boyfriend's hand. All well and good, but I'd rather stay in touch with you directly.'

Annabeth smirked. 'You're right. Can't trust boys to communicate.'

They exchanged cell-phone numbers.

'Just don't call unless it's urgent,' Annabeth warned. 'Cell-phone activity attracts monsters.'

Sadie looked surprised. 'Really? Never noticed. I suppose I shouldn't send you any funny-face selfies on Instagram, then.'

'Probably not.'

'Well, until next time.' Sadie threw her arms round Annabeth.

Annabeth was a little shocked to be getting a hug from a girl she'd just met – a girl who could just as easily have seen Annabeth as an enemy. But the gesture made her feel good. In life-and-death situations, Annabeth had learned, you could make friends pretty quickly.

She patted Sadie's shoulder. 'Stay safe.'

'Hardly ever.' Sadie climbed in her boat, and it pushed out to sea. Fog rose out of nowhere, thickening around the vessel.

When the mist cleared, the ship and Sadie Kane were gone.

Annabeth stared at the empty ocean. She thought about the Mist and the Duat and how they were connected.

Mostly she thought about the staff of Serapis, and the howl the black dog had made when she'd stabbed it with her dagger.

'That wasn't my future I destroyed,' she assured herself. 'I make my own future.'

But somewhere out there a magician named Setne had other ideas. If Annabeth was going to stop him, she had planning to do.

She turned and set out across the beach, heading east on the long journey back to Camp Half-Blood.

THE
CROWN
OF
PTOLEMY

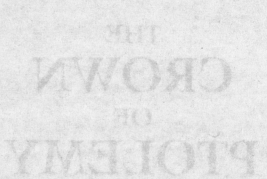

'CARTER!' I SHOUTED.

Nothing happened.

Next to me, pressed against the wall of the old fort, Annabeth peered into the rain, waiting for magical teenagers to fall out of the sky.

'Are you doing it right?' she asked me.

'Gee, I dunno. I'm pretty sure his name is pronounced *Carter*.'

'Try tapping the hieroglyph multiple times.'

'That's stupid.'

'Just try it.'

I stared at my hand. There wasn't even a trace of the hieroglyph that Carter Kane had drawn on my palm almost two months back. He'd assured me that the magic couldn't be washed away, but, with my luck, I'd accidentally wiped it off on my jeans or something.

I tapped my palm. 'Carter. Hello, Carter. Percy to Carter. Paging Carter Kane. Testing, one, two, three. Is this thing on?'

Still nothing.

Usually I wouldn't panic if the cavalry failed to show. Annabeth and I had been in a lot of bad situations without any backup. But usually we weren't stranded on Governors Island in the middle of a hurricane, surrounded by fire-breathing death snakes.

(Actually, I *have* been surrounded by fire-breathing death snakes before, but not ones with wings. Everything is worse when it has wings.)

'All right.' Annabeth wiped the rain out of her eyes, which didn't help, since it was pouring buckets. 'Sadie's not answering her phone. Carter's hieroglyph isn't working. I guess we have to do this ourselves.'

'Sure,' I said. 'But what do we do?'

I peeked around the corner. At the far end of an arched entryway, a grass courtyard stretched about a hundred yards square, surrounded by redbrick buildings. Annabeth had told me this place was a fort or something from the Revolutionary War, but I hadn't listened to the details. Our main problem was the guy standing in the middle of the lawn doing a magic ritual.

He looked like a runty Elvis Presley, strutting back and forth in skinny black jeans, a powder-blue dress shirt and a black leather jacket. His greasy pompadour hairdo seemed impervious to the rain and the wind.

In his hands he held an old scroll, like a treasure map. As he paced, he read aloud from it, occasionally throwing back his head and laughing. Basically the dude was in full-on crazy mode.

If that wasn't creepy enough, flying around him were half a dozen winged serpents, blowing flames in the rain.

Overhead, lightning flashed. Thunder shook my molars.

Annabeth pulled me back.

'That's got to be Setne,' she said. 'The scroll he's reading from is the Book of Thoth. Whatever spell he's casting, we have to stop him.'

At this point I should probably back up and explain what the heck was going on.

Only problem: I wasn't sure what the heck was going on.

A couple of months ago, I fought this giant crocodile on Long Island. A kid named Carter Kane showed up, said he was a magician and proceeded to help me by blowing up stuff with hieroglyphs and turning into a giant glowing chicken-headed warrior. Together we defeated the crocodile, which Carter explained was a son of Sobek, the Egyptian crocodile god. Carter postulated that some strange Egyptian–Greek hybrid stuff was happening. (Gee, I never would've guessed.) He wrote a magical hieroglyph on my hand and told me to call his name if I ever needed help.

Fast-forward to last month: Annabeth ran into Carter's sister, Sadie Kane, on the A train to Rockaway. They fought some godly dude named Serapis, who had a three-headed staff, and a cereal bowl for a hat. Afterwards, Sadie told Annabeth that an ancient magician named Setne might be behind all the weirdness. Apparently this Setne had come back from the dead, snagged an ultra-powerful sorcery cheat sheet called the Book of Thoth and was playing around with Egyptian and Greek magic, hoping to find a way to become a god himself. Sadie and Annabeth had exchanged numbers and agreed to keep in touch.

Today, four weeks later, Annabeth showed up at my apartment at ten in the morning and announced that she'd had a bad dream – a vision from her mom.

(By the way: her mom is Athena, the goddess of wisdom. My dad is Poseidon. We're Greek demigods. Just thought I should mention that, you know, in passing.)

Annabeth decided that, instead of going to the movies, we should spend our Saturday slogging down to the bottom of Manhattan and taking the ferry to Governors Island, where Athena had told her that trouble was brewing.

As soon as we got there, a freak hurricane slammed into New York Harbor. All the mortals evacuated Governors Island, leaving Annabeth and me stranded at an old fort with Crazy Elvis and the Flying Death Snakes.

Make sense to you?

Me neither.

'Your invisibility cap,' I said. 'It's working again, right? How about I distract Setne while you sneak up behind him? You can knock the book out of his hands.'

Annabeth knitted her eyebrows. Even with her blonde hair plastered to the side of her face, she looked cute. Her eyes were the same colour as the storm clouds.

'Setne is supposedly the world's greatest magician,' she said. 'He might be able to see through invisibility. Plus, if you run out there, he'll probably zap you with a spell. Believe me, Egyptian magic is not something you want to get zapped with.'

'I know. Carter walloped me with a glowing blue fist once. But unless you have a better idea . . .'

Unfortunately, she didn't offer one. She pulled her New York Yankees cap from her backpack. 'Give me a minute's head start. Try to take out those flying snakes first. They should be softer targets.'

'Got it.' I raised my ballpoint pen, which doesn't sound like an impressive weapon, but it turns into a magic sword when I uncap it. No, seriously. 'Will a Celestial bronze blade kill them?'

Annabeth frowned. 'It should. At least . . . my bronze dagger worked on the staff of Serapis. Of course, that bronze dagger was made from an Egyptian wand, so . . .'

'I'm getting a headache. Usually when I get a headache it's time to stop talking and attack something.'

'Fine. Just remember: our main goal is to get that scroll. According to Sadie, Setne can use it to turn himself immortal.'

'Understood. No bad guys turning immortal on my watch.' I kissed her, because 1) when you're a demigod going into battle, every kiss might be your last, and 2) I like kissing her. 'Be careful.'

She put on her Yankees cap and vanished.

I'd love to tell you that I walked in and killed the snakes, Annabeth stabbed Elvis in the back and took his scroll, and we went home happy.

You'd figure *once* in a while things would work out the way we planned.

But noooooo.

I gave Annabeth a few seconds to sneak into the courtyard.

Then I uncapped my pen, and Riptide sprang to full length – three feet of razor-sharp Celestial bronze. I strolled into the courtyard and sliced the nearest serpent out of the air.

Nothing says *Hi, neighbour!* like killing a guy's flying reptile.

The snake didn't disintegrate like most monsters I'd fought. Its two halves just landed in the wet grass. The half with wings flopped around aimlessly.

Crazy Elvis didn't notice. He kept pacing back and forth, engrossed in his scroll, so I moved further into the courtyard and sliced another snake.

The storm made it hard to see. Normally I can stay dry when submersed in water, but rain is trickier. It needled my skin and got in my eyes.

Lightning flashed. By the time my vision cleared, two more snakes were dive-bombing me from either side. I jumped backwards just as they blew fire.

FYI, jumping backwards is hard when you're holding a sword. It's even harder when the ground is muddy.

Long story short: I slipped and landed on my butt.

Flames shot over my head. The two snakes circled above me like they were too surprised to attack again. Probably they were wondering, *Did that guy just fall on his butt on purpose? Should we laugh before we kill him? Would that be mean?*

Before they could decide what to do, Crazy Elvis called out, 'Leave him!'

The snakes darted off to join their brethren, who were orbiting ten feet above the magician.

I wanted to get up and face Setne, but my rear end had other ideas. It wanted to stay where it was and be in extreme pain. Butts are like that sometimes. They can be, well, butts.

Setne rolled up his scroll. He sauntered towards me, the rain parting around him like a bead curtain. His winged snakes followed, their flames making plumes of steam in the storm.

'Hi, there!' Setne sounded so casual and friendly I knew I was in trouble. 'You're a demigod, I suppose?'

I wondered how Setne knew that. Maybe he could 'smell' a demigod's aura the way Greek monsters could. Or maybe my prankster friends the Stoll brothers had written I'M A

DEMIGOD on my forehead in permanent marker and Annabeth had decided not to tell me. That happened occasionally.

Setne's smile made his face look even gaunter. Dark eyeliner rimmed his eyes, giving him a hungry, feral stare. Around his neck glittered a golden chain of interlocking ankhs, and from his left ear dangled an ornament that looked like a human finger bone.

'You must be Setne.' I managed to get to my feet without killing myself. 'Did you get that outfit at the Halloween Store?'

Setne chuckled. 'Look, nothing personal, but I'm a little busy at the moment. I'm going to ask you and your girlfriend to wait while I finish my incantation, okay? Once I've summoned the *deshret*, we can chat.'

I tried to look confused, which is one of my most convincing expressions. 'What girlfriend? I'm alone. Also, why are you summoning a dishrag?'

'It's *deshret*.' Setne patted his pompadour. 'The red crown of Lower Egypt. As for your girlfriend . . .'

He wheeled and pointed behind him, shouting something like '*Sun-AH!*'

Red hieroglyphs burned in the air where Setne pointed:

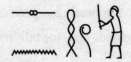

Annabeth turned visible. I'd never actually seen her wearing her Yankees cap before, since she vanished every time she put it on, but there she was – wide-eyed with surprise, caught in the act of sneaking up on Setne.

Before she could react, the red glowing hieroglyphs turned into ropes like liquorice whips and lashed out, wrapping around her, pinning her arms and legs with such force that she toppled over.

'Hey!' I yelled. 'Let her go!'

The magician grinned. 'Invisibility magic. *Please*. I've been using invisibility spells since the pyramids were under warranty. Like I said, this is nothing personal, demigods. I just can't spare the energy to kill you . . . at least not until the summons is over. I hope you understand.'

My heart hammered. I'd seen Egyptian magic before, when Carter helped me fight the giant crocodile on Long Island, but I had no idea how to stop it, and I couldn't stand to see it used against Annabeth.

I charged at Setne. He just waved his hand and muttered, '*Hu-Ai*.'

More stupid hieroglyphs flashed in front of me.

I fell on my face.

My face did not appreciate that. I got mud in my nostrils and blood in my mouth from biting my tongue. When I blinked, the red hieroglyphs burned on the insides of my eyelids.

I groaned. 'What was *that* spell?'

'*Fall*,' Setne said. 'One of my favourites. Don't get up. You'll just hurt yourself more.'

'Setne!' Annabeth shouted through the storm. 'Listen to me. You *can't* make yourself into a god. It won't work. You'll just destroy –'

The coil of magical red ropes expanded, covering Annabeth's mouth.

'I appreciate your concern,' said the magician. 'Really, I do. But I've got this figured out. That business with Serapis . . . when you destroyed my hybrid god? I learned quite a bit from that. I took excellent notes.'

Annabeth struggled uselessly.

I wanted to run to her, but I had a feeling I'd just end up

with my face in the mud again. I'd have to play this smart . . . which was not my usual style.

I tried to steady my breathing. I scooted sideways, just to see if I could.

'So you were watching in Rockaway Beach?' I asked Setne. 'When Annabeth and Sadie took down Serapis, that was all an experiment to you?'

'Of course!' Setne looked very pleased with himself. 'I jotted down the incantations Serapis used while he tried to raise his new Alexandrian lighthouse. Then it was just a matter of cross-referencing those with the older magic in the Book of Thoth, and *voilà*! I found exactly the spell combo I need to make myself into a god. It's going to be great. Watch and see!'

He opened his scroll and started chanting again. His winged serpents spiralled through the rain. Lightning flashed. The ground rumbled.

On Setne's left, about fifteen feet away from me, the grass split open. A geyser of flames spewed upward, and the winged serpents flew straight into it. Earth, fire, rain and serpents swirled into a tornado of elements, merging and solidifying into one huge shape: a coiled cobra with a female human head.

Her reptilian hood was easily six feet across. Her eyes glittered like rubies. A forked tongue flickered between her lips, and her dark hair was plaited with gold. Resting on her head was a sort of crown – a red pillbox-looking thing with a curlicue ornament on the front.

Now, personally, I'm not fond of huge snakes, especially ones with human heads and stupid hats. If I'd summoned this thing, I would've cast a spell to send it back, super quick.

But Setne just rolled up his scroll, slipped it in his jacket pocket and grinned. 'Awesome!'

The cobra lady hissed. 'Who dares summon me? I am Wadjet, queen of cobras, protector of Lower Egypt, eternal mistress of –'

'I know!' Setne clapped his hands. 'I'm a huge fan!'

I crawled towards Annabeth. Not that I could help much with the *fall* spell keeping me off my feet, but I wanted to be close to her if something went down with this eternal cobra queen of whatever, blah, blah, blah. Maybe I could at least use Riptide to cut those red cords and give Annabeth a fighting chance.

'Oh, this is so great,' Setne continued. He fished something out of his jeans . . . a cell phone.

The goddess bared her fangs. She sprayed Setne with a cloud of green mist – poison, I guessed – but he repelled it like the nose cone of a rocket repelled heat.

I kept crawling towards Annabeth, who was struggling helplessly in her red-liquorice cocoon. Her eyes blazed with frustration. She hated being sidelined worse than just about anything.

'Okay, where's the camera icon?' Setne fumbled with his phone. 'We have to get a picture together before I destroy you.'

'*Destroy me?*' demanded the cobra goddess. She lashed out at Setne, but a sudden gust of rain and wind pushed her back.

I was ten feet away from Annabeth. Riptide's blade glowed as I dragged it through the mud.

'Let's see.' Setne tapped his phone. 'Sorry, this is new to me. I'm from the Nineteenth Dynasty. Ah, okay. No. Darn it. Where did the screen go? Ah! Right! So what do modern folks call this . . . a snappie?' He leaned in towards the cobra goddess, held out his phone at arm's length and took a picture. 'Got it!'

'WHAT IS THE MEANING OF THIS?' Wadjet roared. 'YOU DARE TAKE A SELFIE WITH THE COBRA GODDESS?'

'Selfie!' said the magician. 'That's right! Thanks. And now

I'll take your crown and consume your essence. Hope you don't mind.'

'*WHAT?*' The cobra goddess reared and bared her fangs again, but the rain and wind restrained her like a seat belt. Setne shouted something in a mixture of Egyptian and Ancient Greek. A few of the Greek words I understood: *soul* and *bind* and possibly *butter* (though I could be wrong about the last one). The cobra goddess began to writhe.

I reached Annabeth just as Setne finished his spell.

The cobra goddess imploded, with a noise like the world's largest straw finishing the world's largest milkshake. Wadjet was sucked into her own red crown, along with Setne's four winged serpents and a five-foot-wide circle of lawn where Wadjet had been coiled.

The crown dropped into the smoking, muddy crater.

Setne laughed in delight. 'PERFECT!'

I had to agree, if by *perfect* he meant *so horrifying I want to vomit and I have to get Annabeth out of here right now.*

Setne clambered into the pit to retrieve the crown as I frantically started cutting Annabeth's bonds. I'd only managed to ungag her mouth before the bindings blared like an air horn.

My ears popped. My vision went black.

When the sound died and my vertigo faded, Setne was standing over us, the red crown now atop his pompadour.

'The ropes scream if you cut them,' he advised. 'I guess I should've mentioned that.'

Annabeth wriggled, trying to free her hands. 'What – what did you do to the cobra goddess?'

'Hmm? Oh.' Setne tapped the curlicue at the front of the crown. 'I devoured her essence. Now I have the power of Lower Egypt.'

'You . . . devoured a god,' I said.

'Yep!' From his jacket, he pulled the Book of Thoth and wagged it at us. 'Amazing what kind of knowledge is in here. Ptolemy the First had the right idea, making himself a god, but by the time he became king of Alexandria Egyptian magic was diluted and weak. He definitely didn't have access to prime source material like the Book of Thoth. With this baby, I'm cooking with spice! Now that I've got the crown of Lower Egypt –'

'Let me guess,' Annabeth said. 'You'll go for the crown of Upper Egypt. Then you'll put them together and rule the world.'

He grinned. 'Smart girl. But first I have to destroy you two. Nothing personal. It's just that when you're doing hybrid Greek–Egyptian magic I've found that a little demigod blood is a great catalyst. Now, if you'll just hold still –'

I lunged forward and jabbed him with my sword.

Amazingly, Riptide went straight into his gut.

I so rarely succeed that I just crouched there, stunned, my hand trembling on the hilt.

'Wow.' Setne looked down at the blood on his powder-blue shirt. 'Nice job.'

'Thanks.' I tried to yank out Riptide, but it seemed to be stuck. 'So . . . you can die now, if it's not too much trouble.'

Setne smiled apologetically. 'About that . . . I'm beyond dying now. At this point –' He tapped the blade. 'Get it? *This point?* I'm afraid all you can do is make me stronger!'

His red crown began to glow.

For once, my instincts saved my life. Despite the klutz spell Setne had hexed me with, I somehow managed to get to my feet, grab Annabeth and haul her as far from the magician as possible.

I dropped to the ground at the archway as a massive roar shook the courtyard. Trees were uprooted. Windows shattered. Bricks peeled off the wall, and everything in sight hurtled towards Setne as if he'd become the new centre of gravity. Even Annabeth's magical bonds were stripped away. It took all my strength to hold her with one arm while gripping the corner of the building with my other hand.

Clouds of debris spun around the magician. Wood, stone and glass vaporized as they were absorbed into Setne's body.

Once gravity returned to normal, I realized I'd left something important behind.

Riptide was gone. The wound in Setne's gut had closed.

'HEY!' I got up, my legs shaking. 'You ate my sword!'

My voice sounded shrill – like a little kid who's just had his lunch money stolen. The thing is, Riptide was my most important possession. I'd had it a long time. It had seen me through a lot of scrapes.

I'd lost my sword before on a few occasions, but it always reappeared in pen form back in my pocket. I had a feeling that wasn't going to happen this time. Riptide had been *consumed* – sucked into Setne's body along with the bricks, the broken glass and several cubic feet of sod.

Setne turned up his palms. 'Sorry about that. I'm a growing deity. I need my nutrition . . .' He tilted his head as if listening to something in the storm. '*Percy Jackson.* Interesting. And your friend, Annabeth Chase. You two have had some interesting adventures. You'll give me lots of nourishment!'

Annabeth struggled to her feet. 'How do you know our names?'

'Oh, you can learn a lot about someone from devouring their prized possession.' Setne patted his stomach. 'Now, if you don't mind, I really need to consume you both. Not to worry, though! Your essence will live forever right here . . . next to my, uh, pancreas, I think.'

I slipped my hand into Annabeth's. After all we'd been through, I was not going to let our lives end this way – devoured by a wannabe Elvis god with a pillbox hat.

I weighed my options: direct attack or strategic retreat. I wanted to punch Setne in his heavily mascaraed eyes, but if I could get Annabeth to the shore we could jump into the harbour. Being the son of Poseidon, I'd have the upper hand underwater. We could regroup, maybe come back with a few dozen demigod friends and some heavy artillery.

Before I could decide, something completely random changed the equation.

A full-sized camel dropped out of the sky and crushed Setne flat.

'Sadie!' Annabeth cried.

For a split second, I thought she was calling the camel

Sadie. Then I realized Annabeth was looking up into the storm, where two falcons spiralled above the courtyard.

The camel bellowed and farted, which made me appreciate it even more.

Unfortunately we didn't have time to become friends. The camel widened its eyes, bleated in alarm and dissolved into sand.

Setne rose from the dust pile. His crown was tilted. His black jacket was covered in camel fuzz, but he looked unhurt.

'That was rude.' He glanced up at the two falcons now diving towards him. 'No time for this nonsense.'

Just as the birds were about to rip his face off, Setne vanished in a swirl of rain.

The falcons landed and morphed into two human teens. On the right stood my buddy Carter Kane, looking casual in his beige linen combat jammies, with a curved ivory wand in one hand and a crescent-bladed sword in the other. On the left stood a slightly younger blonde girl, who I assumed was his sister, Sadie. She had black linen jammies, orange highlights in her hair, a white wooden staff and mud-spattered combat boots.

Physically, the two siblings looked nothing alike. Carter's complexion was coppery, his hair black and curly. His thoughtful scowl radiated seriousness. By contrast, Sadie was fair-skinned with blue eyes and a lopsided smile so full of mischief I would've figured her for a Hermes kid back at Camp Half-Blood.

Then again, I have Cyclopes and two-tailed mermen as siblings. I wasn't about to comment on the Kane kids' lack of resemblance.

Annabeth exhaled with relief. 'I am *so* glad to see you.'

She gave Sadie a big hug.

Carter and I looked at each other.

'Hey, man,' I said. 'I'm not going to hug you.'

'That's okay,' Carter said. 'Sorry we're late. This storm was messing up our locator magic.'

I nodded like I knew what *locator magic* was. 'So this friend of yours, Setne . . . he's kind of a dirt wipe.'

Sadie snorted. 'You don't know the *half* of it. Did he happen to give you a helpful villain monologue? Reveal his evil plans, say where he was going next, that sort of thing?'

'Well, he used that scroll, the Book of Thoth,' I said. 'He summoned a cobra goddess, devoured her essence and stole her red hat.'

'Oh dear.' Sadie glanced at Carter. 'The crown of Upper Egypt will be next.'

Carter nodded. 'And if he manages to put the two crowns together –'

'He'll become immortal,' Annabeth guessed. 'A newly made god. Then he'll start vacuuming up all the Greek and Egyptian magic in the world.'

'Also he stole my sword,' I said. 'I want it back.'

The three of them stared at me.

'What?' I said. 'I like my sword.'

Carter hooked his curvy-bladed *khopesh* and his wand to his belt. 'Tell us everything that happened. Details.'

While we talked, Sadie muttered some sort of spell, and the rain bent around us like we were under a giant invisible umbrella. Neat trick.

Annabeth had the better memory, so she did most of the explaining about our fight with Setne . . . though calling it a *fight* was generous.

When she was done, Carter knelt and traced some hieroglyphs in the mud.

'If Setne gets the *hedjet*, we're finished,' he said. 'He'll form the crown of Ptolemy and –'

'Hold up,' I said. 'Low tolerance for confusing names. Can you explain what's going on in, like, regular words?'

Carter frowned. 'The *pschent* is the double crown of Egypt, okay? The bottom half is the red crown, the *deshret*. It represents the Lower Kingdom. The top half is the *hedjet*, the white crown of the Upper Kingdom.'

'You wear them together,' Annabeth added, 'and that means you're the pharaoh of all Egypt.'

'Except in this case,' Sadie said, 'our ugly friend Setne is creating a very special *pschent* – the crown of Ptolemy.'

'Okay . . .' I still didn't get it, but felt like I should at least pretend to follow along. 'But wasn't Ptolemy a Greek dude?'

'Yes,' Carter said. 'Alexander the Great conquered Egypt. Then he died. His general Ptolemy took over and tried to mix Greek and Egyptian religion. He proclaimed himself a god-king, like the old pharaohs, but Ptolemy went a step further. He used a combination of Greek and Egypt magic to try making himself immortal. It didn't work out, but –'

'Setne has perfected the formula,' I guessed. 'That Book of Thoth gives him some primo magic.'

Sadie clapped for me. 'I think you've got it. Setne will recreate the crown of Ptolemy, but this time he'll do it properly, and he'll become a god.'

'Which is bad,' I said.

Annabeth tugged thoughtfully at her ear. 'So . . . who was that cobra goddess?'

'Wadjet,' Carter said. 'The guardian of the red crown.'

'And there's a guardian of the white crown?' she asked.

'Nekhbet.' Carter's expression turned sour. 'The vulture goddess. I don't like her much, but I suppose we'll have to stop her from getting devoured. Since Setne needs the Upper Kingdom crown, he'll probably go south for the next ritual. It's like a symbolic thing.'

'Isn't up usually north?' I asked.

Sadie smirked. 'Oh, that would be *much* too easy. In Egypt, up is south, because the Nile runs from the south to the north.'

'Great,' I said. 'So how far south are we talking about – Brooklyn? Antarctica?'

'I don't think he'll go that far.' Carter rose to his feet and scanned the horizon. 'Our headquarters are in Brooklyn. And I'm guessing Manhattan is like Greek god central? A long time ago, our Uncle Amos hinted at that.'

'Well, yeah,' I said. 'Mount Olympus hovers over the Empire State Building, so –'

'Mount Olympus –' Sadie blinked – 'hovers over the . . . Of course it does. Why not? I think what my brother's trying to say is that if Setne wants to establish a new seat of power, blending Greek *and* Egyptian –'

'He'd find a place in between Brooklyn and Manhattan,'

Annabeth said. 'Like right here, Governors Island.'

'Exactly,' Carter said. 'He'll need to conduct the ritual for the second crown south of this point, but it doesn't have to be *far* south. If I were him –'

'And we're glad you're not,' I said.

'– I would stay on Governors Island. We're at the north end now, so . . .'

I gazed south. 'Anyone know what's at the other end?'

'I've never been here,' Annabeth said. 'But I think there's a picnic area.'

'Lovely.' Sadie raised her staff. The tip flared with white fire. 'Anyone fancy a picnic in the rain?'

'Setne's dangerous,' Annabeth said. 'We can't just go charging in. We need a plan.'

'She's right,' Carter said.

'I kind of like charging in,' I said. 'Speed is of the essence, right?'

'*Thank* you,' Sadie muttered.

'Being smart is *also* of the essence,' Annabeth said.

'Exactly,' Carter said. 'We have to figure out how to attack.'

Sadie rolled her eyes at me. 'Just as I feared. These two together . . . they'll overthink us to death.'

I felt the same way, but Annabeth was getting that

annoyed stormy look in her eyes and, since I *date* Annabeth, I figured I'd better suggest a compromise.

'How about we plan while we walk?' I said. 'We can charge south, like, really slowly.'

'Deal,' said Carter.

We headed down the road from the old fort, past some fancy brick buildings that might have been officers' quarters back in the day. We made our way across a soggy expanse of soccer fields. The rain kept pouring down, but Sadie's magic umbrella travelled with us, keeping the worst of the storm away.

Annabeth and Carter compared notes from the research they'd done. They talked about Ptolemy and the mixing of Greek and Egyptian magic.

As for Sadie, she didn't appear interested in strategy. She leaped from puddle to puddle in her combat boots. She hummed to herself, twirled like a little kid and occasionally pulled random things out of her backpack: wax animal figurines, some string, a piece of chalk, a bright yellow bag of candy.

She reminded me of someone . . .

Then it occurred to me. She looked like a younger version of Annabeth, but her fidgeting and hyperness reminded me of . . . well, me. If Annabeth and I ever had a daughter, she might be a lot like Sadie.

Whoa.

It's not like I'd never dreamed about kids before. I mean, you date someone for over a year, the idea is going to be in the back of your mind somewhere, right? But still – I'm barely seventeen. I'm not ready to think *too* seriously about stuff like that. Also, I'm a demigod. On a day-to-day basis, I'm busy just trying to stay alive.

Yet, looking at Sadie, I could imagine that someday maybe I'd have a little girl who looked like Annabeth and acted like me – a cute little hellion of a demigod, stomping through puddles and flattening monsters with magic camels.

I must have been staring, because Sadie frowned at me. 'What?'

'Nothing,' I said quickly.

Carter nudged me. 'Were you listening?'

'Yes. No. What?'

Annabeth sighed. 'Percy, explaining things to you is like lecturing a gerbil.'

'Hey, Wise Girl, don't start with me.'

'Whatever, Seaweed Brain. We were just saying that we'll have to combine our attacks.'

'Combine our attacks . . .' I patted my pocket, but Riptide had not reappeared in pen form. I didn't want to admit how nervous that made me.

Sure, I had other skills. I could make waves (literally) and occasionally even whip up a nice frothy hurricane. But my sword was a big part of who I was. Without it, I felt crippled.

'How do we do combined attacks?'

Carter got a mischievous gleam in his eyes that made him look more like his sister. 'We turn Setne's strategy against him. He's using hybrid magic – Greek and Egyptian together, right? We do the same.'

Annabeth nodded. 'Greek-style attacks won't work. You saw what Setne did with your sword. And Carter is pretty sure regular Egyptian spells won't be enough, either. But if we can find a way to mix our powers –'

'Do you *know* how to mix our powers?' I asked.

Carter's shoes squished in the mud. 'Well . . . not exactly.'

'Oh, please,' Sadie said. 'That's *easy*. Carter, give your wand to Percy.'

'Why?'

'Just do it, brother dear. Annabeth, do you remember when we fought Serapis?'

'Right!' Annabeth's eyes lit up. 'I grabbed Sadie's wand and it turned into a Celestial bronze dagger, just like my old one. It was able to destroy Serapis's staff. Maybe we can create another Greek weapon from an Egyptian wand. Good idea, Sadie.'

'Cheers. You see, I don't need to spend hours planning and researching to be brilliant. Now, Carter, if you please.'

As soon as I took the wand, my hand clenched like I'd grabbed an electrical cable. Spikes of pain shot up my arm. I tried to drop the wand, but I couldn't. Tears filled my eyes.

'By the way,' Sadie said, 'this may hurt a bit.'

'Thanks.' I gritted my teeth. 'Little late on the warning.'

The ivory began to smoulder. When the smoke cleared and the agony subsided, instead of a wand I was holding a Celestial bronze sword that *definitely* wasn't Riptide.

'What is this?' I asked. 'It's huge.'

Carter whistled under his breath. 'I've seen those in museums. That's a *kopis*.'

I hefted the sword. Like so many I'd tried, it didn't feel right in my hands. The hilt was too heavy for my wrist. The single-edged blade was curved awkwardly, like a giant hook knife. I tried a jab and nearly lost my balance.

'This one doesn't look like yours,' I told Carter. 'Isn't yours called a *kopis*?'

'Mine is a *khopesh*,' Carter said. 'The original Egyptian version. What you're holding is a *kopis* – a Greek design adapted from the Egyptian original. It's the kind of sword Ptolemy's warriors would've used.'

I looked at Sadie. 'Is he trying to confuse me?'

'No,' she said brightly. 'He's confusing *without* trying.'

Carter smacked his palm against his forehead. 'That wasn't even confusing. How was that –? Never mind. Percy, the main thing is, can you fight with that sword?'

I sliced the *kopis* through the air. 'I feel like I'm fencing with a meat cleaver, but it'll have to do. What about weapons for you guys?'

Annabeth rubbed the clay beads on her necklace, the way she does when she's thinking. She looked beautiful. But I digress.

'Sadie,' she said, 'those hieroglyphic spells you used on Rockaway Beach . . . which one made the explosion?'

'It's called – well, I can't actually say the word without making you blow up. Hold on.' Sadie rummaged through her backpack. She brought out a sheet of yellow papyrus, a stylus and a bottle of ink – I guess because pen and paper would be un-Egyptian. She knelt, using her backpack as a makeshift writing desk, and scrawled in normal letters: *HA-DI*.

'That's a good spell,' Carter agreed. 'We could show you the hieroglyph for it, but unless you know how to speak words of power –'

'No need,' Annabeth said. 'The phrase means *explode*?'

'More or less,' Sadie said.

'And you can write the hieroglyph on a scroll without triggering the *ka-boom*?'

'Right. The scroll will store the magic for later. If you read the word from the papyrus . . . well, that's even better. More *ka-boom* with less effort.'

'Good,' Annabeth said. 'Do you have another piece of papyrus?'

'Annabeth,' I said, 'what are you doing? 'Cause if you're messing around with exploding words –'

'Relax,' she said. 'I know what I'm doing. Sort of.'

She knelt next to Sadie, who gave her a fresh sheet of papyrus.

Annabeth took the stylus and wrote something in Ancient Greek:

Κεραυνόω

Being dyslexic, I'm lucky if I can recognize *English* words, but, being a demigod, Ancient Greek is sort of hardwired into my brain.

'Ke-rau-noh,' I pronounced. '*Blast?*'

Annabeth gave me a wicked little smile. 'Closest term I could think of. Literally it means *strike with lightning bolts.*'

'Ooh,' Sadie said. 'I love striking things with lightning bolts.'

Carter stared at the papyrus. 'You're thinking we could invoke an Ancient Greek word the same way we do with hieroglyphs?'

'It's worth a try,' Annabeth said. 'Which of you is better with that kind of magic?'

'Sadie,' Carter said. 'I'm more a combat magician.'

'Giant-chicken mode,' I remembered.

'Dude, my avatar is a *falcon-headed warrior.*'

'I still think you could get a sponsorship deal with KFC. Make some big bucks.'

'Knock it off, you two.' Annabeth handed her scroll to Sadie. 'Carter, let's trade. I'll try your *khopesh*; you try my Yankees cap.'

She tossed him the hat.

'I'm usually more of a basketball guy, but . . .' Carter

put on the cap and disappeared. 'Wow, okay. I'm invisible, aren't I?'

Sadie applauded. 'You've never looked better, brother dear.'

'Very funny.'

'If you can sneak up on Setne,' Annabeth suggested, 'you might be able to take him by surprise, get the crown away from him.'

'But you told us Setne saw right through your invisibility,' Carter said.

'That was *me*,' Annabeth said, 'a Greek using a Greek magic item. For you, maybe it'll work better – or differently, at least.'

'Carter, give it a shot,' I said. 'The only thing better than a giant chicken man is a giant invisible chicken man.'

Suddenly the ground shook under our feet.

Across the soccer fields, towards the south end of the island, a white glow lit the horizon.

'That can't be good,' Annabeth said.

'No,' Sadie agreed. 'Perhaps we should charge in a little more quickly.'

The vultures were having a party.

Past a line of trees, a muddy field stretched to the edge of the island. At the base of a small lighthouse, a few picnic tables huddled as if for shelter. Across the harbour, the Statue of Liberty glowed white in the storm, rainclouds pushing around her like waves off the prow of a ship.

In the middle of the picnic grounds, six large black buzzards whirled in the rain, orbiting our buddy Setne.

The magician was rocking a new outfit. He'd changed into a red quilted smoking jacket – I guess to match his red crown. His silk trousers shimmered in red and black paisley. Just to make sure his look wasn't too understated, his loafers were entirely covered in rhinestones.

He strutted around with the Book of Thoth, chanting some spell, the same way he'd done back at the fort.

'He's summoning Nekhbet,' Sadie murmured. 'I'd really rather not see *her* again.'

'What kind of name is Neck Butt, anyway?' I asked.

Sadie snickered. 'That's what *I* called her the first time I saw her. But, really, she's *not* very nice. Possessed my gran, chased me across London . . .'

'So what's the plan?' Carter asked. 'Maybe a flanking manoeuvre?'

'Or,' Annabeth said, 'we could try a diversionary –'

'Charge!' Sadie barrelled into the clearing, her staff in one hand and her Greek scroll in the other.

I glanced at Annabeth. 'Your new friend is awesome.'

Then I followed Sadie.

My plan was pretty simple: run at Setne and kill him. Even with my heavy new sword, I outpaced Sadie. Two vultures dived at me. I sliced them out of the air.

I was five feet from Setne and imagining the satisfaction of slicing him in half when he turned and noticed me. The magician vanished. My blade cut through empty air.

I stumbled, off-balance and angry.

Ten feet to my left, Sadie smacked a vulture with her staff. The bird exploded into white sand. Annabeth jogged towards us, giving me one of those annoyed expressions like, *If you get yourself killed, I'm going to murder you.* Carter, being invisible, was nowhere to be seen.

With a bolt of white fire, Sadie blasted another vulture out of the sky. The remaining birds scattered in the storm.

Sadie scanned the field for Setne. 'Where *is* the skinny old git?'

The skinny old git appeared right behind her. He spoke a single word from his scroll of nasty surprises, and the ground exploded.

When I regained my senses, I was still standing, which was a minor miracle. The force of the spell had pushed me away from Setne, so my shoes had made trenches in the mud.

I looked up, but I couldn't make sense of what I was seeing. Around Setne, the earth had ruptured in a ten-foot-diameter ring, splitting open like a seedpod. Plumes of dirt had sprayed outwards and were frozen in midair. Tendrils of red sand coiled around my legs and brushed against my face as they snaked in all directions. It looked like somebody had stopped time while slinging red mud from a giant salad spinner.

Sadie lay flat on the ground to my left, her legs buried under a blanket of mud. She struggled but couldn't seem to get free. Her staff was knocked out of reach. Her scroll was a muddy rag in her hand.

I stepped towards her, but the coils of sand pushed me back.

Somewhere behind me, Annabeth yelled my name. I turned and saw her just outside the explosion zone. She was trying to charge in, but the earthen tendrils moved to block her, whipping around like octopus arms.

There was no sign of Carter. I could only hope he hadn't got caught in this stupid web of floating dirt.

'Setne!' I yelled.

The magician brushed the lapels of his smoking jacket. 'You *really* should stop interrupting me, demigod. The *deshret* crown was originally a gift to the pharaohs from the earth god Geb, you know. It can defend itself with some cool earth magic!'

I gritted my teeth. Annabeth and I had recently done battle with Gaia the Earth Mother. More dirt sorcery was the *last* thing I needed.

Sadie struggled, her legs still encased in mud. 'Clean up all this dirt right now, young man. Then give us that crown and go to your room.'

The magician's eyes glittered. 'Ah, Sadie. Delightful as always. Where's your brother? Did I accidentally blow him up? You can thank me for that later. Right now, I must get on with business.'

He turned his back on us and resumed chanting.

The wind picked up. Rain whipped around him. The floating lines of sand began to stir and shift.

I managed to step forward, but it was like wading through wet cement. Behind me, Annabeth wasn't having much more luck. Sadie managed to pull one of her legs free, minus her combat boot. She cursed worse than my immortal horse friend Arion (which is pretty bad) as she retrieved the boot.

Setne's weird earth spell was loosening, but not fast enough. I'd only managed two more steps when Setne finished his incantation.

In front of him, a wisp of darkness grew into the form of a queenly woman. Rubies embroidered the collar of her black dress. Gold bands circled her upper arms. Her face had an imperious, timeless quality that I'd learned to recognize. It meant *I'm a goddess; deal with it.* Perched atop her braided black hair was a white conical crown, and I couldn't help wondering why a powerful immortal being would choose to wear a headpiece shaped like a bowling pin.

'You!' she snarled at Setne.

'Me!' he agreed. 'Wonderful to see you again, Nekhbet. Sorry we don't have longer to chat, but I can't keep these mortals pinned down forever. We'll have to make this brief. The *hedjet*, please.'

The vulture goddess spread her arms, which grew into huge black wings. Around her, the air turned dark as smoke. 'I do not yield to upstarts like you. I am the protector of the crown, the shield of the pharaoh, the –'

'Yes, yes,' Setne said. 'But you've yielded to upstarts plenty of times. The history of Egypt is basically a list of which upstarts you've yielded to. So let's have the crown.'

I didn't know vultures could hiss, but Nekhbet did. Smoke billowed from her wings.

All around the clearing, Setne's earth magic shattered.

The tendrils of red sand fell to the ground with a loud *slosh*, and suddenly I could move again. Sadie struggled to her feet. Annabeth ran to my side.

Setne didn't seem concerned about us.

He gave Nekhbet a mock bow. 'Very impressive. But watch this!'

He didn't need to read from the scroll this time. He shouted a combination of Greek and Egyptian – words I recognized from the spell he'd used back at the fort.

I locked eyes with Annabeth. I could tell we were thinking the same thing. We couldn't let Setne consume the goddess.

Sadie raised her muddy piece of papyrus. 'Annabeth, you and Percy get Nekhbet out of here. GO!'

No time to argue. Annabeth and I ploughed into the goddess like linebackers and pushed her across the field, away from Setne.

Behind us, Sadie yelled, '*Ke-rau-noh!*'

I didn't see the explosion, but it must have been impressive.

Annabeth and I were thrown forward. We landed on top of Nekhbet, who let out an indignant squawk. (By the way, I would not recommend stuffing your pillow with vulture feathers. They're not very comfy.)

I managed to get up. Where Setne had been standing was a smoking crater.

Sadie's hair was singed at the tips. Her scroll was gone. Her eyes were wide with surprise. 'That was brilliant. Did I get him?'

'Nope!' Setne appeared a few feet away, stumbling a little. His clothes were smouldering, but he looked more dazed than hurt.

He knelt and picked up something conical and white . . . Nekhbet's crown, which must've rolled off when we tackled her.

'Thanks for this.' Setne spread his arms triumphantly – the white crown in one hand, the Book of Thoth in the other. 'Now, where was I? Oh, right! Consuming all of you!'

Across the field, Carter's voice yelled: '*STAHP!*'

I guess *stahp* is actually a word in Ancient Egyptian. Who knew?

A bright blue hieroglyph scythed through the air, cutting off Setne's right hand at the wrist.

Setne shrieked in pain. The Book of Thoth dropped into the grass.

Twenty feet away from me, Carter appeared out of thin air, holding Annabeth's Yankees cap. He wasn't in giant-chicken mode, but, since he'd just saved our lives, I wasn't going to complain.

Setne glanced down at the Book of Thoth, still in his severed hand, but I lunged forward, thrusting the point of my new sword under his nose. 'I don't think so.'

The magician snarled. 'Take the book, then! I don't need it any more!'

He vanished in a whirl of darkness.

On the ground behind me, the vulture goddess Nekhbet thrashed and pushed Annabeth aside. 'Get off me!'

'Hey, lady –' Annabeth rose – 'I was trying to keep you from being devoured. You're welcome.'

The vulture goddess got to her feet.

She didn't look nearly as impressive without her crown. Her hairdo was a mud-and-grass salad. Her black dress had turned into a smock of moulting feathers. She looked shrivelled and hunched over, with her neck sticking out like . . . well, a vulture. All she needed was a cardboard sign saying, HOMELESS, ANYTHING HELPS, and I totally would have given her my spare change.

'You miserable children,' she grumbled. 'I could have destroyed that magician!'

'Not so much,' I said. 'A few minutes ago, we watched Setne inhale a cobra goddess. She was a lot more impressive than you.'

Nekhbet's eyes narrowed. 'Wadjet? He inhaled *Wadjet*? Tell me everything.'

Carter and Sadie joined us as we briefed the goddess on what had happened so far.

When we were done, Nekhbet wailed in outrage. 'This is unacceptable! Wadjet and I were the symbols of unity in Ancient Egypt. We were revered as the Two Ladies! That upstart Setne has stolen my other Lady!'

'Well, he didn't get you,' Sadie said. 'Which I suppose is a good thing.'

Nekhbet bared her teeth, which were pointy and red like a row of little vulture beaks. 'You *Kanes*. I should've known you'd be involved. Always mucking about in godly affairs.'

'Oh, so now it's *our* fault?' Sadie hefted her staff. 'Listen here, buzzard breath –'

'Let's stay focused,' Carter said. 'At least we got the Book of Thoth. We stopped Setne from devouring Nekhbet. So what's Setne's next move, and how do we stop him?'

'He has both parts of the *pschent*!' said the vulture goddess. 'Without my essence, the white crown is not as powerful as it would be, true, but it's still enough for Setne's purposes. He needs only to complete the deification ceremony while wearing the crown of Ptolemy. Then he will become a god. I *hate* it when mortals become gods! They always want thrones. They build garish McPalaces. They don't respect the rules in the gods' lounge.'

'The gods' lounge?' I asked.

'We must stop him!' Nekhbet yelled.

Sadie, Carter, Annabeth and I exchanged uneasy looks. Normally when a god says, *We must stop him*, it means, *You must stop him while I sit back and enjoy a cold beverage*. But Nekhbet seemed serious about joining the gang.

That didn't make me any less nervous. I try to avoid teaming up with goddesses who eat roadkill. It's one of my personal boundaries.

Carter knelt. He pulled the Book of Thoth from Setne's severed hand. 'Can we use the scroll? It has powerful magic.'

'If that's true,' Annabeth said, 'why would Setne leave it behind? I thought it was the key to his immortality.'

'He said he was done with it,' I recalled. 'I guess he, like, passed the test, so he threw away his notes.'

Annabeth looked horrified. 'Are you crazy? You throw away your notes after a test?'

'Doesn't everybody, Miss Brainiac?'

'Guys!' Sadie interrupted. 'It's terribly cute watching you two snipe at each other, but we have business.' She turned to Nekhbet. 'Now, your Scavenging Highness, is there a way to stop Setne?'

Nekhbet curled her talon fingernails. 'Possibly. He's not a full god yet. But, without my crown, my own powers are greatly diminished.'

'What about the Book of Thoth?' Sadie asked. 'It may be no further use to Setne, but it *did* help us defeat Apophis.'

At the mention of that name, Nekhbet's face blanched. Three feathers fell from her dress. 'Please don't remind me of that battle. But you're correct. The Book of Thoth contains a spell for imprisoning gods. It would take a great deal of concentration and preparation . . .'

Carter coughed. 'I'm guessing Setne won't stand around quietly while we get ready.'

'No,' Nekhbet agreed. 'At least three of you would be required to set a proper trap. A circle must be drawn. A rope must be enchanted. The earth must be consecrated. Other parts of the spell would have to be improvised. I hate Ptolemaic magic. Mixing Greek and Egyptian power is an abomination. However –'

'It works,' Annabeth said. 'Carter was able to go invisible using my hat. Sadie's explosion scroll at least dazed Setne.'

'But we'll need more,' Sadie said.

'Yes . . .' The vulture goddess fixed her eyes on me like I was a tasty dead possum on the side of the highway. 'One of you will have to fight Setne and keep him unbalanced while the others prepare the trap. We need a very potent hybrid attack, an abomination even Ptolemy would approve of.'

'Why are you looking at me?' I asked. 'I'm not abominable.'

'You are a son of Poseidon,' the goddess noted. 'That would be a most unexpected combination.'

'Combination? What –'

'Oh, no, no, no.' Sadie raised her hands. She looked horrified, and anything that could scare *that* girl I did not want to know about. 'Nekhbet, you can't be serious. You want a demigod to host you? He's not even a magician. He doesn't have the blood of the pharaohs!'

Carter grimaced. 'That's her point, Sadie. Percy isn't the

usual kind of host. If the pairing worked, he could be very powerful.'

'Or it could melt his brain!' Sadie said.

'Hold it,' Annabeth said. 'I prefer my boyfriend with an unmelted brain. What exactly are we talking about here?'

Carter wagged the Yankees cap at me. 'Nekhbet wants Percy to be her host. That's one way the Egyptian gods maintain a presence in the mortal world. They can inhabit mortals' bodies.'

My stomach jackknifed. 'You want *her* –' I pointed at the frazzled old vulture goddess – 'to *inhabit* me? That sounds . . .'

I tried to think of a word that would convey my complete disgust without offending the goddess. I failed.

'Nekhbet –' Annabeth stepped forward – 'join with me instead. I'm a child of Athena. I might be better –'

'Ridiculous!' The goddess sneered. 'Your mind is too wily, girl – too stubborn and intelligent. I couldn't steer you as easily.'

'*Steer* me?' I protested. 'Hey, lady, I'm not a Toyota.'

'My host needs a certain level of simplicity,' the goddess continued. 'Percy Jackson is perfect. He is powerful, yet his mind is not overly crowded with plans and ideas.'

'Wow,' I said. 'Really feeling the love here.'

Nekhbet rounded on me. 'There is no time to argue! Without a physical anchor, I cannot remain in the mortal world much longer. If you want to stop Setne from becoming immortal, you need the power of a god. We must act *now*. Together, we will triumph! We will feast upon that upstart magician's carcass!'

I swallowed. 'I'm actually trying to cut back on carcass feasting.'

Carter gave me a sympathetic look that only made me feel worse. 'Unfortunately, Nekhbet is right. Percy, you're our best shot. Sadie and I couldn't host Nekhbet even if she wanted us to. We already have patron gods.'

'Who, conveniently, have gone silent,' Sadie noted. 'Scared of getting their essences sucked up, I suppose.'

Nekhbet fixed her glittery black eyes on me. 'Do you consent to hosting me, demigod?'

I could think of a million ways to say no. The word *yes* simply wouldn't pass my lips. I glanced at Annabeth for support, but she looked as alarmed as I felt.

'I – I don't know, Percy,' she confessed. 'This is *way* beyond me.'

Suddenly the rainstorm fizzled out. In the eerie muggy quiet, a red glow lit the middle of the island, as if somebody had started a bonfire on the soccer fields.

'That would be Setne,' Nekhbet said. 'He has begun his ascension to godhood. What is your answer, Percy Jackson? This will only work properly if you consent.'

I took a deep breath. I told myself that hosting a goddess couldn't be worse than all the other weird horrible things I'd experienced in my demigod career . . . Besides, my friends needed my help. And I did not want that skinny Elvis impersonator to become a god and build a McPalace in my neighbourhood.

'All right,' I said. 'Vulture me up.'

Nekhbet dissolved into black smoke. She swirled around me – filling my nostrils with a smell like boiling tar.

What was it like merging with a god?

If you want the full details, read my Yelp review. I don't feel like going into it again. I gave the experience half a star.

For now, let's just say that being possessed by a vulture goddess was even more disturbing than I'd imagined.

Thousands of years of memories flooded my mind. I saw pyramids rising from the desert, the sun glittering on the River Nile. I heard priests chanting in the cool shadows of a temple and smelled myrrh incense on the air. I soared over the cities of Ancient Egypt, circling the palace of the pharaoh. I was the vulture goddess Nekhbet – protector of the king, shield of the strong, scourge of the weak and dying.

I also had a burning desire to find a nice warm hyena carcass, stick my face right in there and –

Okay, basically I wasn't myself.

I tried to focus on the present. I stared at my shoes . . . the same old pair of Brooks, yellow shoelace on the left, black shoelace on the right. I raised my sword arm to make sure I could still control my muscles.

Relax, demigod. The voice of Nekhbet spoke in my mind. *Let me take charge.*

'I don't think so,' I said aloud. I was relieved that my voice still sounded like my voice. 'We do this together or not at all.'

'Percy?' Annabeth asked. 'Are you okay?'

Looking at her was disorientating. The 'Percy' part of me saw my usual awesome girlfriend. The 'Nekhbet' part of me saw a young woman surrounded by a powerful ultraviolet aura – the mark of a Greek demigod. The sight filled me with disdain and fear. (For the record: I have my own healthy fear of Annabeth. She has kicked my butt on more than one occasion. But disdain? Not so much. That was all Nekhbet.)

'I'm fine,' I said. 'I was talking to the vulture in my head.'

Carter walked a circle around me, frowning like I was an abstract sculpture. 'Percy, try to strike a balance. Don't let her take over, but don't fight her, either. It's kind of like running a three-legged race. You have to get in a rhythm with your partner.'

'But if you have to choose,' Sadie said, 'smack her down and stay in control.'

I snarled. 'Stupid girl! Do not tell me –' I forced my lips closed. The taste of rotting jackal filled my mouth. 'Sorry, Sadie,' I managed. 'That was Nekhbet talking, not me.'

'I know.' Sadie's expression tightened. 'I wish we had more time for you to get used to hosting a goddess. However –'

Another red flash illuminated the treetops.

'The sooner I get this goddess out of my head, the better,' I said. 'Let's go smash Setne's face.'

Setne really could not decide on his wardrobe.

He strutted around the soccer field in black bell-bottomed slacks, a frilly white shirt and a glittery purple trench coat – all of which clashed with his newly combined red and white crown. He looked like Prince from one of my mom's old album covers, and, judging from the magic lights swirling around him, Setne was getting ready to party like it was 1999 B.C.E.

Having only one hand didn't seem to bother him. He waved his stump conductor-style, chanting in Greek and Egyptian while fog rose at his feet. Bursts of light danced and bobbed around him, as if a thousand kids were writing their names with sparklers.

I didn't understand what I was looking at, but Nekhbet did. Having her sight, I recognized the Duat – the magical dimension that existed beneath the mortal realm. I saw layers of reality, like strata of glowing multicoloured jelly, plunging down into infinity. On the surface, where the mortal and immortal worlds met, Setne was whipping the Duat into a storm – churning waves of colour and frothy white plumes of smoke.

After Annabeth's adventure on Rockaway Beach, she'd told me how frightening it was to see the Duat. She wondered whether the Egyptian Duat was somehow related to the Greek concept of Mist – the magical veil that kept mortals from recognizing gods and monsters.

With Nekhbet in my mind, I knew the answer. Of course

the Mist was related. The Mist was simply a Greek name for the uppermost layer between the worlds – the layer that Setne was now shredding.

I should have been terrified. Seeing the world in all its infinite levels was enough to give anybody vertigo.

But I'd been dropped into oceans before. I was used to floating in the depths with endless thermal layers around me.

Also, Nekhbet wasn't easily impressed. She'd seen just about everything over the millennia. Her mind was as cold and dry as the desert night wind. To her, the mortal world was a constantly changing wasteland, dotted with the carcasses of men and their civilizations. Nothing lasted. It was all roadkill waiting to happen. As for the Duat, it was always churning, sending up plumes of magic like sun flares into the mortal world.

Still, we were both disturbed by the way Setne's spell tore through the Mist. He wasn't just manipulating it. Magicians did that all the time. Setne was strip-mining the Duat. Wherever he stepped, fractures radiated outwards, cleaving through the layers of the magic realm. His body sucked in energy from every direction, destroying the boundaries between the Duat and the mortal world, between Greek magic and Egyptian magic – slowly transforming him into an immortal. In the process, he was ripping a hole in the cosmic order that might never close.

His magic pulled at us – Nekhbet and me – urging us to give up and be absorbed into his new glorious form.

I didn't want to be absorbed. Neither did the vulture goddess. Our common purpose helped us work together.

I marched across the field. Sadie and Annabeth fanned out on my right. I assumed Carter was somewhere on my left, but he'd gone invisible again, so I couldn't be sure. The fact that I couldn't detect him, even with Nekhbet's super vulture senses, gave me hope that Setne wouldn't see him, either.

Maybe if I kept Setne busy, Carter would be able to cut off Setne's other hand. Or his legs. Bonus points for his head.

Setne stopped chanting when he saw me.

'Awesome!' He grinned. 'You brought the vulture with you. Thanks!'

Not the reaction I'd been hoping for. I keep waiting for the day when the bad guy sees me and screams, *I give up!* But it hasn't happened yet.

'Setne, drop the crown.' I raised my *kopis*, which didn't feel heavy with Nekhbet's power flowing through me. 'Surrender, and you might get out of this alive. Otherwise –'

'Oh, very good! Very threatening! And your friends

here . . . Let me guess. You keep me occupied while they set some amazing trap to contain the newly made god?'

'You're not a god yet.'

He waved off the comment. 'I suppose Carter is lurking around here too, all stealthy and invisible? Hi, Carter!'

If Carter was nearby, he didn't respond. Smart guy.

Setne raised his stump of a wrist. 'Wherever you are, Carter, I was impressed with the hand-cutting-off spell. Your father would be proud. That's what matters to you, isn't it? Making your father proud? But think what would be possible if you joined me. I intend to change the rules of the game. We could bring your father back to life – I mean *real* life, not that horrible half life he's got in the Underworld. Anything is possible once I'm a god!'

Around Setne's wrist, the Mist curled, solidifying into a new hand. 'What do you say, Carter?'

Above the magician, the air shimmered. A giant blue fist the size of a refrigerator appeared over Setne's head and pounded him into the ground like a nail into soft wood.

'I say no.' Carter appeared across the field, Annabeth's Yankees cap in his hand.

I stared at the crown of Ptolemy – the only part of Setne still visible above ground.

'You were supposed to wait,' I told Carter. 'Set the trap. Let me deal with Setne.'

Carter shrugged. 'He shouldn't have brought up my father.'

'Never mind that!' Annabeth said. 'Get the crown!'

I realized she was right. I would've sprung into action, except Nekhbet and I had a moment of paralysis. The goddess wanted her hat back. But I took one look at the crown's eerie glow, remembered the way the cobra goddess had been devoured and decided I was *not* touching that crown without latex gloves and maybe a hazmat suit.

Before Nekhbet and I could resolve our differences, the earth rumbled.

Setne rose from the ground as if on an elevator platform and glared at Carter. 'I make you a perfectly fair offer, and you hit me with a giant fist? Perhaps your father wouldn't be proud, after all.'

Carter's face contorted. His whole body glowed with blue light. He levitated off the ground as the avatar of Horus took shape around him.

Setne didn't look worried. He curled his newly regrown fingers in a *come here* gesture, and Carter's avatar shattered. The blue light swirled towards Setne and was engulfed in his growing aura. Carter collapsed, motionless, on the wet ground.

'SETNE!' Sadie shouted, raising her staff. 'Over here, you little weasel!'

She blasted the magician with a jet of white fire. Setne caught it on his chest and absorbed the energy.

'Sadie, hon,' he chided. 'Don't be mad. Carter has always been the *boring* one. I didn't really want to grant him eternal life. But you – why don't you work with me, eh? We can have tons of fun! Tearing up the universe, destroying things as we see fit!'

'That's – that's not fair,' Sadie said, her voice trembling. 'Tempting me with destruction.'

She tried for her usual sassy tone, but her eyes stayed fixed on Carter, who still wasn't moving.

I knew I should do something. We'd had a plan . . . But I couldn't remember it. The vulture goddess in my head was flying circles on autopilot. Even Annabeth looked like she was struggling to concentrate. Being so close to Setne was like standing next to a waterfall. His white noise drowned out everything.

'You know,' Setne continued, as if we were planning a party together, 'I think this island will be perfect. My palace will go right here, in the new centre of the universe!'

'A muddy soccer field,' Annabeth noted.

'Oh, come now, child of Athena! You can see the possibilities. That old fool Serapis had the right idea: gather all the wisdom of Greece and Egypt together in one place and use that power to rule the world! Except Serapis didn't have my *vision*. I'll consume the old pantheons – Zeus, Osiris, all those dusty deities. Who needs them? I'll just take the bits and pieces I can use from all of them. I'll become the head of a new race of gods. Humans will come here from all over the world to make offerings and buy souvenirs.'

'Souvenirs?' I said. 'You want immortality so you can sell T-shirts?'

'And snow globes!' Setne got a dreamy look in his eyes. 'I love snow globes. Anyway, there's room for more than one new god. Sadie Kane – you'd be perfect. I know you love breaking rules. Let's break *all* of them! Your friends can come along too!'

Behind the magician, Carter groaned and began to stir.

Setne glanced back with distaste. 'Not dead yet? Tough kid. Well . . . I suppose we can include him in our plans. Although, if you'd prefer, Sadie, I can certainly finish him off.'

Sadie let loose a guttural cry. She advanced, but Annabeth caught her arm.

'Fight smart,' Annabeth said. 'Not angry.'

'Point taken,' Sadie said, though her arms still trembled with rage. 'But I'll do both.'

She unfurled the Book of Thoth.

Setne just laughed. 'Sadie dear, I know how to defeat every spell in that book.'

'You won't win,' Sadie insisted. 'You won't take anything else from anyone!'

She began to chant. Annabeth raised her borrowed *khopesh*, ready to defend her.

'Ah, well.' Setne sighed. 'I suppose you'll want *this* back, then.'

Setne's body began to glow. Thanks to Nekhbet, I realized what was going to happen a split second before it did, which saved our lives.

Carter was just struggling to his feet when I shouted, 'GET DOWN!'

He dropped like a sack of rocks.

A ring of fire exploded outwards from Setne.

I discarded my sword and lunged in front of the girls, spreading my arms goalie-style. A shell of purple light surrounded me, and the flames rolled harmlessly over translucent wings that now extended on either side of me.

With my new accessories I was able to shield Sadie and Annabeth from the worst of the blast.

I lowered my arms. The giant wings retracted. My feet, floating just off the ground, were now encased in large ghostly legs with three long toes and the talons of a bird.

When I realized I was hovering at the centre of a giant glowing purple vulture, my first thought was: *Carter will never stop teasing me about this.*

My second thought was: *Oh, gods. Carter.*

Sadie must have seen him at the same time I did. She screamed.

The fire had blackened the entire field, instantly turning wet mud into cracked clay. The Mist and magic lights had burned away. My new sword was a steaming line of bronze slag on the ground. Carter lay right where he'd dropped, wreathed in smoke, his hair charred, his face red with blisters.

I feared the worst. Then his fingers twitched. He croaked out a sound, like '*Gug*', and I could breathe again.

'Thank the gods,' Annabeth said.

Setne brushed some ash off his purple trench coat. 'Well, you can thank the gods if you want, but they won't be around

much longer. Another few minutes and the magic I've started
will be irreversible. Now, Percy, please drop that silly avatar
before I take it away from you. And, Sadie, I suggest you give
me the Book of Thoth before you hurt yourself. There's no
spell you could read that would harm me.'

Sadie stepped forward. Her orange-highlighted hair
whipped around her face. Her eyes turned steely, making her
look even more like a young Annabeth.

'No spell *I* could read,' Sadie agreed. 'But I have friends.'

She handed the Book of Thoth to Annabeth, who blinked
in surprise. 'Um . . . Sadie?'

Setne chuckled. 'What's *she* going to do? She may be
smart, but she can't read Old Egyptian.'

Sadie gripped Annabeth's forearm. 'Miss Chase,' she said
formally, 'I have one word for you.' She leaned in and
whispered something in Annabeth's ear.

Annabeth's face transformed. Only once before had I seen
her with such an expression of pure wonder: when she beheld
the gods' palaces on Mount Olympus.

Sadie turned to me. 'Percy . . . Annabeth has work to do. I
need to tend to my brother. Why don't you keep our friend
Setne entertained?'

Annabeth opened the scroll. She began to read aloud in

Ancient Egyptian. Glowing hieroglyphs floated off the papyrus. They swirled in the air around her, mixing with Greek words as if Annabeth was adding her own commentary to the spell.

Setne looked even more surprised than I was. He made a strangled noise in the back of his throat. 'That's not . . . Hold on now. No!'

He raised his arms to cast some counter spell. His crown began to glow.

I needed to move, but Nekhbet wasn't helping. She was a little too focused on Carter, who smelled chargrilled and yummy.

That one is weak, she murmured in my mind. *Dead soon. The weak must die.*

Anger gave me the upper hand. Carter Kane was my friend. I would *not* sit around while my friend died.

Move, I told Nekhbet. And I took control of the vulture avatar.

Before Setne could finish casting his spell, I grabbed him in my spectral claws and carried him into the sky.

Now . . . I live and breathe weirdness. It goes with the territory when you're a demigod. But there are still moments when I do a mental double take: like when I'm flying upward inside a giant glowing vulture, flapping my arms to control make-believe wings, holding an almost-immortal magician in my talons . . . all so I can steal his hat.

That hat was not coming off, either.

I spiralled into the storm, shaking Setne, trying to knock the crown off his head, but the dude must have fastened it to his pompadour with superglue.

He blasted me with fire and flashes of light. My bird exoskeleton deflected the attacks, but, each time, the purple avatar dimmed, and my wings felt heavier.

'Percy Jackson!' Setne writhed in my claws. 'This is a waste of time!'

I didn't bother responding. The strain of combat was quickly taking its toll.

During our first encounter, Carter had warned me that magic could literally burn up a magician if he used too much at once. I guessed that applied to demigods, too. Every time Setne blasted me or tried to wriggle out of my grip with his near-godly strength, my head throbbed. My eyesight dimmed. Soon I was drenched in sweat.

I hoped Sadie was helping Carter. I hoped Annabeth was finishing whatever super-weird spell she'd been chanting so we could trap Setne, because I couldn't stay airborne much longer.

We broke through the top of the cloud layer. Setne stopped fighting, which surprised me so much I almost dropped him. Then coldness began to seep through my vulture avatar, chilling my wet clothes, soaking into my bones. It was a subtler kind of attack – probing for weakness – and I knew I couldn't allow it. I curled my vulture feet tighter around Setne's chest, hoping to crush him.

'Percy, Percy.' His tone made it sound like we were a couple of bros on a night out. 'Don't you see what an incredible opportunity this is? A perfect *do-over*. You of all people should appreciate that. The Olympians once offered you their most valuable gift. They offered to make you a god, didn't they? And you – you lovable idiot – you turned them down! This is your chance to correct that mistake.'

My avatar flickered and blinked like a bad fluorescent tube. Nekhbet, my brain buddy, turned her attention inward.

You turned down immortality? Her voice was incredulous, offended.

She scanned my memories. I saw my own past from her dry, cynical point of view: I stood in the throne room of Mount Olympus after the war against the Titans. Zeus offered me a reward: godhood. I turned him down flat. I wanted justice for other demigods instead. I wanted the gods to stop being jerks and to pay attention to their kids.

A stupid request. A naive thing to wish for. I gave up power. You *never* give up power.

I struggled to keep my grip on Setne. 'Nekhbet, those are *your* thoughts, not mine. I made the right choice.'

Then you are a fool, the vulture goddess hissed.

'Yeah, pal,' Setne said, who apparently could hear her. 'I gotta agree with Nekhbet on this one. You did the noble thing. How did that work out? Did the gods honour their promises?'

I couldn't separate Nekhbet's bitterness from my own feelings. Sure, I grumbled about the gods all the time, but I'd never regretted my decision to stay mortal. I had a girlfriend. I had a family. I had my whole life ahead of me – assuming I could stay alive.

Now . . . maybe it was just Nekhbet in my mind, or Setne toying with me, but I started to wonder if I'd made a huge blunder.

'I get it, kid.' Setne's voice was full of pity. 'The gods are your family. You want to think they're good. You want to make them proud. I wanted that with *my* family. My dad was Ramses the Great, you know.'

I was gliding in a lazy circle now, my left wing carving the tops of the storm clouds. Setne's crown glowed more brightly. His aura grew colder, numbing my limbs and turning my thoughts sluggish. I knew I was in trouble, but I couldn't think of what to do about it.

'It's hard having a powerful dad,' Setne continued. 'Ramses was the pharaoh, of course, so most of the time he was hosting the god Horus. That made him distant, to say the least. I kept thinking, *If I just make the right choices and prove I'm a good kid, he'll eventually notice me. He'll treat me right.* But, the thing is, the gods don't care about mortals, even their children. Look into the vulture's mind if you don't believe me. Behave like a good little boy, act all noble – that just makes it easier for the gods to ignore you. The only way to get their respect is to act up, be *bad* and take what you want!'

Nekhbet didn't try to convince me otherwise. She was the protector goddess of the pharaohs, but she didn't care about them as individual humans. She cared about maintaining the power of Egypt, which in turn kept the worship of the gods alive. She certainly didn't care about noble acts or fairness. Only the weak demanded fairness. The weak were carcasses waiting to die – appetizers in the long dinner of Nekhbet's eternal life.

'You're a good kid,' Setne told me. 'A lot nicer than the goddess you're trying to host. But you've got to see the truth. You should've taken Zeus's offer. You would be a god now. You'd be strong enough to *make* those changes you asked for!'

Strength is good, Nekhbet agreed. *Immortality is good.*

'I'm giving you a second chance,' Setne said. 'Help me out, Percy. Become a god.'

We turned in the air as Nekhbet's consciousness separated from mine. She'd forgotten which of us was the enemy. Nekhbet favoured the strong. Setne was strong. I was weak.

I remembered the way Setne had been strip-mining the Duat – cutting fissures in reality, destroying the entire cosmic order to make himself immortal.

I'll just take the bits and pieces I can use, he'd told Sadie.

My thoughts finally cleared. I understood how Setne operated, how he'd beaten us so badly up till now.

'You're looking for a way into my mind,' I said. 'Something you can relate to and use against me. But I'm not like you. I don't *want* immortality, especially not if it rips the world apart.'

Setne smiled. 'Well, it was worth a try. Especially since I made you lose control of your vulture!'

An explosion of cold shattered my avatar. Suddenly I was falling.

My one advantage: I'd been holding Setne in my claws, which meant he was directly below me. I slammed right into him and locked my arms around his chest. We plummeted together through the clouds.

I shivered so badly that I was surprised I could stay conscious. Frost caked my clothes. Wind and ice stung my eyes. I felt like I was downhill skiing without a mask.

I'm not sure why Setne didn't just magic himself away. I suppose even a powerful magician can succumb to panic. When you're free-falling, you forget to think rationally: *Gee, I have spells and stuff.* Instead your animal brain takes over and you think: *OH MY GOD THIS KID IS HOLDING ON TO ME AND I'M TRAPPED AND FALLING AND I'M GOING TO DIE!*

Even though I was seconds away from becoming vulture hors d'oeuvres, Setne's squawking and flapping brought me some satisfaction.

If we'd fallen straight down, I would've hit solid ground and died. No question.

Fortunately, the winds were strong and Governors Island was a small target in a very big harbour.

We hit the water with a wonderfully familiar *KA-FLOOM!*

My pain disappeared. Warmth surged back into my limbs.

Salt water swirled around me, filling me with new energy. Seawater always did good things for me, but normally not this fast. Maybe the presence of Nekhbet ramped up my healing. Maybe my dad Poseidon was trying to do me a favour.

Whatever the case, I felt great. I grabbed Setne by the throat with one hand and began to squeeze. He fought like a demon. (Believe me, I know. I've fought a few.) The crown of Ptolemy glowed in the water, steaming like a volcanic vent. Setne clawed at my arm and exhaled streams of bubbles – maybe trying to cast spells, or maybe trying to sweet talk me out of strangling him. I couldn't hear him, and I didn't want to. Underwater, I was in charge.

Bring him to shore, said Nekhbet's voice.

Are you crazy? I thought back. *This is my home court.*

He cannot be defeated here. Your friends are waiting.

I didn't want to, but I understood. I might be able to keep Setne occupied underwater for a while, but he was too far down the path to immortality for me to destroy. I needed to undo his magic, which meant I needed help.

I kept my grip on his throat and let the currents push me to Governors Island.

Carter waited for me on the island's ring road. His head was wrapped in bandages like a turban. The blisters on his face had been treated with some kind of purple goo. His linen ninja jammies looked like they'd been laundered in a burning wood chipper. But he was alive, and angry. In one hand he held a glowing white rope like a cowboy's lasso.

'Welcome back, Percy.' He glared at Setne. 'This guy give you any trouble?'

Setne flailed and shot fire in Carter's direction. Carter lashed the flames aside with his rope.

'I've got him under control for now,' I said.

I felt confident that was true. The seawater had brought me back to full strength. Nekhbet was cooperating again, ready to shield me from anything Setne might try. The magician himself seemed dazed and deflated. Getting strangled at the bottom of New York Harbor will do that to you.

'Let's go, then,' Carter said. 'We have a nice reception planned.'

Back at the burnt soccer fields, Sadie and Annabeth had sketched a magical bull's-eye on the ground. At least that's how it looked to me. The chalk circle was about five feet in diameter and elaborately bordered with words of power in Greek and hieroglyphics. In the Duat, I could see that the circle radiated white light. It was drawn over the rift that

Setne had made, like a bandage over a wound.

The girls stood on opposite sides of the circle. Sadie crossed her arms and planted her combat boots defiantly. Annabeth was still holding the Book of Thoth.

When she saw me, she kept her battle face on, but from the gleam in her eyes I could tell she was relieved.

I mean . . . we'd just passed our one-year dating anniversary. I figured I was a sort of long-term investment for her. She hoped I would pay dividends eventually; if I died now, she would've put up with all my annoying qualities for nothing.

'You lived,' she noted.

'No thanks to Elvis.' I lifted Setne by his neck. He weighed almost nothing. 'He was pretty tough until I figured out his system.'

I threw him into the centre of the circle. The four of us surrounded him. The hieroglyphs and Greek letters burned and swirled, rising in a funnel cloud to contain our prisoner.

'Dude is a scavenger,' I said. 'Not too different from a vulture. He picks through our minds, finds whatever he can relate to, and he uses that to get through our defences. Annabeth's love of wisdom. Carter's desire to make his dad proud. Sadie's –'

'My incredible modesty,' Sadie guessed. 'And obvious good looks.'

Carter snorted.

'Anyway,' I said, 'Setne tried to offer me immortality. He tried to get a handle on my motives for turning it down once before, but –'

'Pardon,' Sadie interrupted. 'Did you say you've turned down immortality before?'

'You can still be a god!' Setne croaked. 'All of you! Together we can –'

'I don't *want* to be a god,' I said. 'You don't get that, do you? You couldn't find anything about me you could relate to, which I take as a big compliment.'

Inside my mind, Nekhbet hissed: *Kill him. Destroy him utterly.*

No, I said. *Because that's not me, either.*

I stepped to the edge of the circle. 'Annabeth, Carter, Sadie . . . you ready to put this guy away?'

'Any time.' Carter hefted his rope.

I crouched until I was face-to-face with Setne. His kohl-lined eyes were wide and unfocused. On his head, the crown of Ptolemy tilted sideways like an observatory telescope.

'You were right about one thing,' I told him. 'There's a lot of power in mixing Greek and Egyptian. I'm glad you introduced me to my new friends. We're going to keep mixing it up.'

'Percy Jackson, listen –'

'But there's a difference between sharing and stealing,' I said. 'You have something that belongs to me.'

He started to speak. I shoved my hand right in his mouth.

Sound gross? Wait, it gets worse.

Something guided me – maybe Nekhbet's intuition, maybe my own instincts. My fingers closed around a small pointy object in the back of Setne's throat, and I yanked it free: my ballpoint pen, Riptide.

It was like I'd pulled the plug out of a tyre. Magic spewed from Setne's mouth: a multicoloured stream of hieroglyphic light.

GET BACK! Nekhbet screamed in my mind as Annabeth yelled the same thing aloud.

I stumbled away from the circle. Setne writhed and spun as all the magic he'd tried to absorb now came gushing out in a disgusting torrent. I'd heard about people 'puking rainbows', because they saw something that was just too cute.

Let me tell you: if you actually *see* someone puking

rainbows . . . there's nothing cute about it.

Annabeth and Sadie shouted magic commands in unison. The funnel cloud of magic intensified around the circle, hemming in Setne, who was shrivelling rapidly. The crown of Ptolemy rolled off his head. Carter stepped forward and threw his glowing rope.

As soon as the rope touched Setne, a flash of light blinded me.

When my vision returned, Setne and the rope were gone. No magic lights swirled. The vulture goddess had left my mind. My mouth no longer tasted like dead hyena.

Annabeth, the Kanes and I stood in a loose ring, staring at the crown of Ptolemy, which lay sideways in the dirt. Next to it sat a plastic bauble the size of a goose egg.

I picked it up.

Inside the snow globe, a miniature model of Governors Island was permanently submerged. Alternately running and swimming around the landscape, trying to avoid flurries of fake snow, was a termite-sized man in a purple trench coat.

Setne had made Governors Island his eternal headquarters, after all.

He'd been imprisoned in a cheap plastic souvenir.

An hour later, we sat on the parapets of the old fort, watching the sun go down over the New Jersey coastline. I'd had a cheese sandwich and an ice-cold Ribena from Sadie's extra-dimensional stash of junk food (along with two extra-strength painkillers), so I was feeling brave enough to hear explanations.

'Would someone explain what happened back there?' I asked.

Annabeth slipped her hand into mine. 'We won, Seaweed Brain.'

'Yeah, but . . .' I gestured at the snow globe, which Carter was now admiring. 'How?'

Carter shook the globe. Fake snow swirled inside. Maybe it was my imagination, but I swear I could hear Setne shrieking underwater as he was given the blender tour of his tiny prison.

'I guess the snow-globe idea got stuck in my head,' Carter said. 'When I threw the rope and sprang the trap, the magic conformed to what I was thinking. Anyway, Setne will make a great paperweight.'

Sadie snorted, almost nostril-spewing her Ribena. 'Poor little Setne – stuck on Carter's desk for eternity, forced to watch him do hours and hours of boring research. It would've been kinder to let Ammit devour his soul.'

I didn't know who Ammit was, but I didn't need any more soul-devouring monsters in my life.

'So the trap worked,' I said, which I guess was kind of obvious. 'I don't need to understand all the details –'

'That's good,' Annabeth said. 'Since I don't think any of us do.'

'– but one thing I've gotta know.' I pointed at Sadie. 'What did you whisper to Annabeth that turned her into a magician?'

The girls exchanged a smile.

'I told Annabeth my secret name,' Sadie said.

'Your what, now?' I asked.

'It's called the *ren*,' Sadie explained. 'Everyone has one, even if you don't know it. The *ren* is . . . well, the definition of who you are. Once I shared it, Annabeth had access to my experiences, my abilities, all my general amazingness.'

'That was risky.' Carter gave me a grim look. 'Anyone who knows your *ren* can control you. You never share that information unless you really have to, and only with people you absolutely trust. Sadie found out my secret name last year. My life has sucked ever since.'

'Oh, please,' Sadie said. 'I only use my knowledge for good.'

Carter suddenly slapped himself in the face.

'Hey!' he complained.

'Oops, sorry,' Sadie said. 'At any rate, I *do* trust Annabeth. I knew it would take both of us to create that containment circle. Besides, a Greek demigod casting Egyptian magic – did you see the look on Setne's face? Priceless.'

My mouth went dry. I imagined Annabeth invoking hieroglyphs at Camp Half-Blood, blowing up chariots on the racetrack, hurling giant blue fists during capture the flag.

'So my girlfriend is a magician now, like, permanently? Because she was scary enough before.'

Annabeth laughed. 'Don't worry, Seaweed Brain. The effect of learning Sadie's *ren* is already wearing off. I'll never be able to do any magic on my own.'

I breathed a sigh of relief. 'Okay. So, um . . . last question.'

I nodded to the crown of Ptolemy, which sat on the parapet next to Sadie. It looked like part of a Halloween costume, not the sort of headgear that could violently rip the world apart. 'What do we do with that?'

'Well,' Sadie said, 'I could put it on and see what happens.'

'NO!' Carter and Annabeth yelled.

'Kidding,' Sadie said. 'Honestly, you two, calm down. I

must admit, though, I don't see why Wadjet and Nekhbet didn't reclaim their crowns. The goddesses *were* freed, weren't they?'

'Yeah,' I said. 'I sensed that cobra lady Wadjet get expelled when Setne was puking rainbows. Then Nekhbet went back to . . . wherever goddesses go when they're not annoying mortals.'

Carter scratched his bandaged head. 'So . . . they just *forgot* their crowns?'

Traces of Nekhbet's personality lingered in the corners of my mind – just enough to make me uncomfortably sure that the crown of Ptolemy had been left here on purpose.

'It's a test,' I said. 'The Two Ladies want to see what we'll do with it. When Nekhbet learned that I'd turned down immortality once before, she was kind of offended. I think she's curious to find out if any of us will go for it.'

Annabeth blinked. 'Nekhbet would do that out of *curiosity*? Even if it caused a world-destroying event?'

'Sounds like Nekhbet,' Sadie said. 'She's a malicious old bird. Loves to watch us mortals squabble and kill each other.'

Carter stared at the crown. 'But . . . we know better than to use that thing. Don't we?' His voice sounded a little wistful.

'For once you're right, brother dear,' Sadie said. 'As much as I'd love to be a literal goddess, I suppose I'll have to remain a *figurative* one.'

'I'm going to puke rainbows now,' Carter said.

'So what do we do with the crown?' Annabeth asked. 'It's not the kind of thing we should leave at the Governors Island Lost and Found.'

'Hey, Carter,' I said, 'after we defeated that crocodile monster on Long Island, you said you had a safe place to keep its necklace. Could you store the crown, too?'

The Kanes had a silent conversation with each other.

'I suppose we could bring the crown to the First Nome in Egypt,' Carter said. 'Our Uncle Amos is in charge there. He has the most secure magic vaults in the world. But nothing is one hundred percent safe. Setne's experiments with Greek and Egyptian magic sent tremors through the Duat. Gods and magicians felt them. I'm sure demigods felt them, too. That kind of power is tempting. Even if we lock the crown of Ptolemy away –'

'Others might try hybrid magic,' Annabeth said.

'And the more it's tried,' Sadie said, 'the more damage could be done to the Duat, and the mortal world, and our sanity.'

We sat in silence as that idea sank in. I imagined what

would happen if the kids in the Hecate cabin back at camp heard about Egyptian magicians in Brooklyn, or if Clarisse from the Ares cabin learned how to summon a giant wild-boar combat avatar.

I shuddered. 'We'll have to keep our worlds separate as much as possible. The info is too dangerous.'

Annabeth nodded. 'You're right. I don't like keeping secrets, but we'll have to be careful who we talk to. Maybe we can tell Chiron, but –'

'I bet Chiron already knows about the Egyptians,' I said. 'He's a wily old centaur. But, yeah. We'll have to keep our little task force here on the down-low.'

'"Our little task force".' Carter grinned. 'I like the sound of that. The four of us can keep in touch. We'll have to stand ready in case something like this happens again.'

'Annabeth has my number,' Sadie said. 'Which, honestly, brother, is a much easier solution than writing invisible hieroglyphs on your friend's hand. What were you thinking?'

'It made sense at the time,' Carter protested.

We cleaned up our picnic stuff and got ready to go our separate ways.

Carter carefully wrapped the crown of Ptolemy in linen

cloth. Sadie gave the Governors Island snow globe a good shake, then stuffed it in her pack.

The girls hugged. I shook Carter's hand.

With a twinge of pain, I realized how much I was going to miss these kids. I was getting tired of making new friends only to tell them goodbye, especially since some of them never came back.

'Take care of yourself, Carter,' I said. 'No more getting roasted in explosions.'

He smirked. 'I can't promise. But call us if you need us, okay? And, uh, thanks.'

'Hey, it was a team effort.'

'I guess. But, Percy . . . it came down to you being a good person. Setne couldn't get a handle on you. Honestly, if I'd been tempted with godhood the way you were tempted –'

'You would've done the same thing,' I said.

'Maybe.' He smiled, but he didn't look convinced. 'Okay, Sadie. Time to fly. The initiates at Brooklyn House are going to be worried.'

'And Khufu is making jelly fruit salad for dinner,' she said. 'Should be delicious. Toodle-oo, demigods!'

The Kanes turned into birds of prey and launched themselves into the sunset.

'This has been a weird day,' I told Annabeth.

She slipped her hand into mine. 'I'm thinking cheese-burgers for dinner at P. J. Clarke's.'

'With bacon,' I said. 'We've earned it.'

'I love the way you think,' she said. 'And I'm glad you're not a god.'

She kissed me, and I decided that I was glad too. A kiss in the sunset and the promise of a good bacon cheeseburger – with that kind of payoff, who needs immortality?

HOW DO YOU PUNISH
AN IMMORTAL?
BY MAKING HIM HUMAN.

Rick Riordan returns to Camp Half-Blood
in his incredible new series!

Read on for a sneak peek
at the first book ...

THE
TRIALS OF
APOLLO
THE HIDDEN ORACLE

Hoodlums punch my face
I would smite them if I could
Mortality blows

MY NAME IS APOLLO. I used to be a god.

In my four thousand, six hundred and twelve years, I have done many things. I inflicted a plague on the Greeks who besieged Troy. I blessed Babe Ruth with three home runs in game four of the 1926 World Series. I visited my wrath upon Britney Spears at the 2007 MTV Video Music Awards.

But in all my immortal life I never before crash-landed in a dumpster.

I'm not even sure how it happened.

I simply woke up falling. Skyscrapers spiralled in and out of view. Flames streamed off my body. I tried to fly. I tried to change into a cloud or teleport across the world or do a hundred other things that should have been easy for me, but I just kept falling. I plunged into a narrow canyon between two buildings and *BAM!*

Is anything sadder than the sound of a god hitting a pile of garbage bags?

I lay groaning and aching in the open dumpster. My nostrils burned with the stench of rancid salami and used diapers. My ribs felt broken, though that shouldn't have been possible.

My mind stewed in confusion, but one memory floated to the surface – the voice of my father Zeus: *YOUR FAULT. YOUR PUNISHMENT.*

I realized what had happened to me. And I sobbed in despair.

Even for a god of poetry such as myself, it is difficult to describe how I felt. How could you – a mere mortal – possibly understand? Imagine being stripped of your clothes, then blasted with a fire hose in front of a laughing crowd. Imagine the ice-cold water filling your mouth and lungs, the pressure bruising your skin, turning your joints to putty. Imagine feeling helpless, ashamed, completely vulnerable – publically and brutally stripped of everything that makes you *you*. My humiliation was worse than that.

YOUR FAULT, Zeus's voice rang in my head.

'No!' I cried miserably. 'No, it wasn't! Please!'

Nobody answered. On either side of me, rusty fire escapes zigzagged up brick walls. Above, the winter sky was grey and unforgiving.

I tried to remember the details of my sentencing. Had my father told me how long this punishment would last? What was I supposed to do to regain his favour?

My memory was too fuzzy. I could barely recall what Zeus looked like, much less why he'd decided to toss me to earth. There'd been a war with the giants, I thought. The gods had been caught off guard, embarrassed, almost defeated.

The only thing I knew for certain: my punishment was unfair. Zeus needed someone to blame, so of course he'd picked the handsomest, most talented, most popular god in the pantheon: me.

I lay in the garbage, staring at the label inside the dumpster lid: FOR PICK-UP, CALL 1-555-STENCHY.

Zeus will reconsider, I told myself. *He's just trying to scare me. Any moment, he will yank me back to Olympus and let me off with a warning.*

'Yes . . .' My voice sounded hollow and desperate. 'Yes, that's it.'

I tried to move. I wanted to be on my feet when Zeus came to apologize. My ribs throbbed. My stomach clenched. I clawed the rim of the dumpster and managed to drag myself over the side. I toppled out and landed on my shoulder, which made a cracking sound against the asphalt.

'*Araggeeddeee,*' I whimpered through the pain. 'Stand up. Stand up.'

Getting to my feet was not easy. My head spun. I almost passed out from the effort. I stood in a dead-end alley. About fifty feet away, the only exit opened onto a street with grimy storefronts for a bail bondsman's office and a pawnshop. I was somewhere on the west side of Manhattan, I guessed, or perhaps Crown Heights, in Brooklyn. Zeus must have been really angry with me.

I inspected my new body. I appeared to be a teenaged Caucasian male, clad in sneakers, blue jeans and a green polo shirt. How utterly *drab.* I felt sick, weak and so, so human.

I will never understand how you mortals tolerate it. You live your entire life trapped in a sack of meat, unable to enjoy simple pleasures like changing into a hummingbird or dissolving into pure light.

And now, heavens help me, I was one of you – just another meat sack.

I fumbled through my pockets, hoping I still had the keys to my sun chariot. No such luck. I found a cheap nylon wallet containing a hundred dollars in American currency – lunch money for my first day as a mortal, perhaps – along with a New York State junior driver's licence featuring a photo of a dorky, curly-haired teen who could not possibly be me, with the name *Lester Papadopoulos*. The cruelty of Zeus knew no bounds!

I peered into the dumpster, hoping my bow, quiver and lyre might have fallen to earth with me. I would have settled for my harmonica. There was nothing.

I took a deep breath. *Cheer up*, I told myself. *I must have retained some of my godly abilities. Matters could be worse.*

A raspy voice called, 'Hey, Cade, take a look at this loser.'

Blocking the alley's exit were two young men: one squat and platinum blond, the other tall and redheaded. Both wore oversized hoodies and baggy jeans. Serpentine tattoo designs covered their necks. All they were missing were the words I'M A THUG printed in large letters across their foreheads.

The redhead zeroed in on the wallet in my hand. 'Now be nice, Mikey. This guy looks friendly enough.' He grinned and pulled a hunting knife from his belt. 'In fact, I bet he wants to give us all his money.'

I blame my disorientation for what happened next.

I knew my immortality had been stripped away, but I still considered myself the mighty Apollo! One cannot change one's way of thinking as easily as one might, say, turn into a snow leopard.

Also, on previous occasions when Zeus had punished me by

making me mortal (yes, it had happened twice before), I retained massive strength and at least some of my godly powers. I assumed the same would be true now.

I was *not* going to allow two young mortal ruffians to take Lester Papadopoulos's wallet.

I stood up straight, hoping Cade and Mikey would be intimidated by my regal bearing and divine beauty. (Surely those qualities could not be taken from me, no matter what my driver's licence photo looked like.) I ignored the warm dumpster juice trickling down my neck.

'I am Apollo,' I announced. 'You mortals have three choices: offer me tribute, flee, or be destroyed.'

I wanted my words to echo through the alley, shake the towers of New York and cause the skies to rain smoking ruin. None of that happened. On the word *destroyed*, my voice squeaked.

The redhead Cade grinned even wider. I thought how amusing it would be if I could make the snake tattoos around his neck come alive and strangle him to death.

'What do you think, Mikey?' he asked his friend. 'Should we give this guy tribute?'

Mikey scowled. With his bristly blond hair, his cruel small eyes and his thick frame, he reminded me of the monstrous sow that terrorized the village of Crommyon back in the good old days.

'Not feeling the tribute, Cade.' His voice sounded like he'd been eating lit cigarettes. 'What were the other options?'

'Fleeing?' said Cade.

'Nah,' said Mikey.

'Being destroyed?'

Mikey snorted. 'How about we destroy *him* instead?'

Cade flipped his knife and caught it by the handle. 'I can live with that. After you.'

I slipped the wallet into my back pocket. I raised my fists. I did not like the idea of flattening mortals into flesh waffles, but I was sure I could do it. Even in my weakened state, I would be far stronger than any human.

'I warned you,' I said. 'My powers are far beyond your comprehension.'

Mikey cracked his knuckles. 'Uh-huh.'

He lumbered towards me.

As soon as he was in range, I struck. I put all my wrath into that punch. It should have been enough to vaporize Mikey and leave a thug-shaped impression on the asphalt.

Instead he ducked, which I found quite annoying.

I stumbled forward. I have to say that when Prometheus fashioned you humans out of clay he did a shoddy job. Mortal legs are clumsy. I tried to compensate, drawing upon my boundless reserves of agility, but Mikey kicked me in the back. I fell on my divine face.

My nostrils inflated like airbags. My ears popped. The taste of copper filled my mouth. I rolled over, groaning, and found the two blurry thugs staring down at me.

'Mikey,' said Cade, 'are you comprehending this guy's power?'

'Nah,' said Mikey. 'I'm not comprehending it.'

'Fools!' I croaked. 'I will destroy you!'

'Yeah, sure.' Cade tossed away his knife. 'But first I think we'll stomp you.'

Cade raised his boot over my face, and the world went black.

THE
GODS OF ASGARD
ARISE!

Magnus Chase, cousin of Annabeth, has
always run away from trouble, but
trouble has a way of finding him . . .

Read on for a sneak peek at the
first adventure in a thrilling new series!

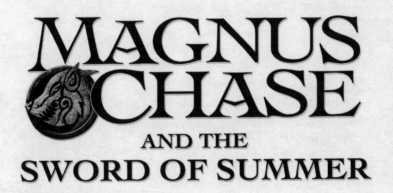

MAGNUS
CHASE
AND THE
SWORD OF SUMMER

Good Morning!
You're Going to Die

YEAH, I KNOW. You guys are going to read about how I died in agony, and you're going be like, 'Wow! That sounds cool, Magnus! Can I die in agony, too?'

No. Just no.

Don't go jumping off any rooftops. Don't run into the highway or set yourself on fire. It doesn't work that way. You will not end up where I ended up.

Besides, you wouldn't want to deal with my situation. Unless you've got some crazy desire to see undead warriors hacking one another to pieces, swords flying up giants' noses and dark elves in snappy outfits, you shouldn't even *think* about finding the wolf-headed doors.

My name is Magnus Chase. I'm sixteen years old. This is the story of how my life went downhill after I got myself killed.

My day started out normal enough. I was sleeping on the sidewalk under a bridge in the Public Garden when a guy kicked me awake and said, 'They're after you.'

By the way, I've been homeless for the past two years.

Some of you may think, *Aw, how sad.* Others may think, *Ha ha, loser!* But, if you saw me on the street, ninety-nine per cent of you would walk right past like I'm invisible. You'd pray, *Don't let him ask me for money.* You'd wonder if I'm older than I look, because surely a teenager wouldn't be wrapped in a stinky old sleeping bag, stuck outside in the middle of a Boston winter. *Somebody should help that poor boy!*

Then you'd keep walking.

Whatever. I don't need your sympathy. I'm used to being laughed at. I'm definitely used to being ignored. Let's move on.

The bum who woke me was a guy called Blitz. As usual, he looked like he'd been running through a dirty hurricane. His wiry black hair was full of paper scraps and twigs. His face was the colour of saddle leather and was flecked with ice. His beard curled in all directions. Snow caked the bottom of his trench coat where it dragged around his feet – Blitz being about five feet five – and his eyes were so dilated the irises were all pupil. His permanently alarmed expression made him look like he might start screaming any second.

I blinked the gunk out of my eyes. My mouth tasted like day-old hamburger. My sleeping bag was warm, and I really didn't want to get out of it.

'Who's after me?'

'Not sure.' Blitz rubbed his nose, which had been broken so many times it zigzagged like a lightning bolt. 'They're handing out flyers with your name and picture.'

I cursed. Random police and park rangers I could deal with. Truant officers, community-service volunteers, drunken college kids, addicts looking to roll somebody small and weak – all those would've been as easy to wake up to as pancakes and orange juice.

But when somebody knew my name and my face – that was bad. That meant they were targeting me specifically. Maybe the folks at the shelter were mad at me for breaking their stereo. (Those Christmas carols had been driving me crazy.) Maybe a security camera had caught that last bit of pickpocketing I did in the Theater District. (Hey, I needed money for pizza.) Or maybe, unlikely as it seemed, the police were still looking for me, wanting to ask questions about my mom's murder . . .

I packed my stuff, which took about three seconds. The sleeping bag rolled up tight and fitted in my backpack with my toothbrush and a change of socks and underwear. Except for the clothes on my back, that's all I owned. With the backpack over my shoulder and the hood of my jacket pulled low, I could blend in with pedestrian traffic pretty well. Boston was full of college kids. Some of them were even more scraggly and younger-looking than me.

I turned to Blitz. 'Where'd you see these people with the flyers?'

'Beacon Street. They're coming this way. Middle-aged white guy and a teenage girl, probably his daughter.'

I frowned. 'That makes no sense. Who –'

'I don't know, kid, but I gotta go.' Blitz squinted at the sunrise, which was turning the skyscraper windows orange. For reasons I'd never quite understood, Blitz hated the daylight. Maybe he was the world's shortest, stoutest homeless vampire. 'You should go see Hearth. He's hanging out in Copley Square.'

I tried not to feel irritated. The local street people jokingly called Hearth and Blitz my mom and dad because one or the other always seemed to be hovering around me.

'I appreciate it,' I said. 'I'll be fine.'

Blitz chewed his thumbnail. 'I dunno, kid. Not today. You gotta be extra careful.'

'Why?'

He glanced over my shoulder. 'They're coming.'

I didn't see anybody. When I turned back, Blitz was gone.

I hated it when he did that. Just – *Poof*. The guy was like a ninja. A homeless vampire ninja.

Now I had a choice: go to Copley Square and hang out with Hearth, or head towards Beacon Street and try to spot the people who were looking for me.

Blitz's description of them made me curious. A middle-aged white guy and a teenage girl searching for me at sunrise on a bitter-cold morning. Why? Who were they?

I crept along the edge of the pond. Almost nobody took the lower trail under the bridge. I could hug the side of the hill and spot anyone approaching on the higher path without them seeing me.

Snow coated the ground. The sky was eye-achingly blue. The bare tree branches looked like they'd been dipped in glass. The wind cut through my layers of clothes, but I didn't mind the cold. My mom used to joke that I was half polar bear.

Dammit, Magnus, I chided myself.

After two years, my memories of her were still a minefield. I'd stumble over one, and instantly my composure would be blown to bits.

I tried to focus.

The man and the girl were coming this way. The man's sandy hair grew over his collar – not like an intentional style, but like he couldn't be bothered to cut it. His baffled expression reminded me of a substitute teacher's: *I know I was hit by a spit wad, but I have no idea where it came from.* His smart shoes were totally wrong for a Boston winter. His socks were different shades of brown. His tie looked like it had been tied while he spun around in total darkness.

The girl was definitely his daughter. Her hair was just as thick and wavy, though lighter blonde. She was dressed more sensibly in snow boots, jeans and a parka, with an orange T-shirt peeking out at the neckline. Her expression was more determined, angry. She gripped a sheaf of flyers like they were essays she'd been graded on unfairly.

If she was looking for me, I did not want to be found. She was scary.

I didn't recognize her or her dad, but something tugged at the back of my skull . . . like a magnet trying to pull out a very old memory.

Father and daughter stopped where the path forked. They looked around as if just now realizing they were standing in the middle of a deserted park at no-thank-you o'clock in the dead of winter.

'Unbelievable,' said the girl. 'I want to strangle him.'

Assuming she meant me, I hunkered down a little more.

Her dad sighed. 'We should probably avoid killing him. He *is* your uncle.'

'But *two years?*' the girl demanded. 'Dad, how could he not tell us for *two years?*'

'I can't explain Randolph's actions. I never could, Annabeth.'

I inhaled so sharply I was afraid they would hear me. A scab was ripped off my brain, exposing raw memories from when I was six years old.

Annabeth. Which meant the sandy-haired man was . . . *Uncle Frederick?*

I flashed back to the last family Thanksgiving we'd shared: Annabeth and me hiding in the library at Uncle Randolph's town house, playing with dominoes while the adults yelled at each other downstairs.

You're lucky you live with your momma. Annabeth stacked another domino on her miniature building. It was amazingly good, with columns in front like a temple. *I'm going to run away.*

I had no doubt she meant it. I was in awe of her confidence.

Then Uncle Frederick appeared in the doorway. His fists were clenched. His grim expression was at odds with the smiling reindeer on his sweater. *Annabeth, we're leaving.*

Annabeth looked at me. Her grey eyes were a little too fierce for a first-grader's. *Be safe, Magnus.*

With a flick of her finger, she knocked over her domino temple.

That was the last time I'd seen her.

Afterwards, my mom had been adamant: *We're staying away from your uncles. Especially Randolph. I won't give him what he wants. Ever.*

She wouldn't explain what Randolph wanted, or what she and Frederick and Randolph had argued about.

You have to trust me, Magnus. Being around them . . . it's too dangerous.

I trusted my mom. Even after her death, I hadn't had any contact with my relatives.

Now, suddenly, they were looking for me.

Randolph lived in town, but, as far as I knew, Frederick and Annabeth still lived in Virginia. Yet here they were, passing out flyers with my name and photo on them. Where had they even *got* a photo of me?

My head buzzed so badly that I missed some of their conversation.

'– to find Magnus,' Uncle Frederick was saying. He checked his smartphone. 'Randolph is at the city shelter in the South End. He says no luck. We should try the youth shelter across the park.'

'How do we even know Magnus is alive?' Annabeth asked miserably. 'Missing for *two years*? He could be frozen in a ditch somewhere!'

Part of me was tempted to jump out of my hiding place and shout, *TA-DA!*

Even though it had been ten years since I'd seen Annabeth, I didn't like seeing her distressed. But after so long on the streets I'd learned the hard way: you never walk into a situation until you understand what's going on.

'Randolph is sure Magnus is alive,' said Uncle Frederick. 'He's somewhere in Boston. If his life is truly in danger . . .'

They set off towards Charles Street, their voices carried away by the wind.

I was shivering now, but it wasn't from the cold. I wanted to run after Frederick, tackle him and demand to hear what was going on. How did Randolph know I was still in town? Why were they looking for me? How was my life in danger now more than on any other day?

But I didn't follow them.

I remembered the last thing my mom ever told me. I'd been reluctant to use the fire escape, reluctant to leave her, but she'd gripped my arms and made me look at her. *Magnus, run. Hide. Don't trust anyone. I'll find you. Whatever you do, don't go to Randolph for help.*

Then, before I'd made it out of the window, the door of our apartment had burst into splinters. Two pairs of glowing blue eyes had emerged from the darkness . . .

I shook off the memory and watched Uncle Frederick and Annabeth walk away, veering east towards the Common.

Uncle Randolph . . . For some reason, he'd contacted Frederick and Annabeth. He'd got them to Boston. All this time, Frederick and Annabeth hadn't known that my mom was dead and I was missing. It seemed impossible, but, if it were true, why would Randolph tell them about it now?

Without confronting him directly, I could think of only one way to get answers. His town house was in Back Bay, an easy walk from here. According to Frederick, Randolph wasn't home. He was somewhere in the South End, looking for me.

Since nothing started a day better than a little breaking and entering, I decided to pay his place a visit.

MAGNUS CHASE

The Gods of Asgard Arise

A breathtaking new series
featuring the gods of Norse mythology

RICK RIORDAN

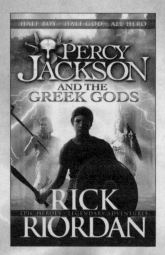
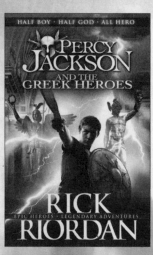